NEW GIRL AT WINSTON HIGH

NEW GIRL AT WINSTON HIGH

by

Arlene Collyer Swanson

Reilly & Lee Co.
Chicago · 1963

To my daughter Susan

My best friend and severest critic

CHAPTER I

Kerry lay prone on the diving board, her arms dangling limply, her finger tips just flicking the motionless surface of the pool. The hot August sun burned into her legs and back and drugged her into a pleasant semi-sleep. Through half-closed eyes she watched the butterflies, like wisps of white tissue, scallop the still, hot air as they swooped among the flowers in the meadow. Befurred bumble bees, drunk with nectar, staggered from wild aster to golden rod. The only sound that penetrated her drowsiness was the faint hum of traffic on the parkway a quarter of a mile away.

She was exhausted. The whole morning and most of the afternoon she had spent mulching the laurel, weeding the delphinium beds, and spraying the taxus. Dad would be surprised tonight when he saw the results. Before he had left for the mountains to dig rhodedendron, he had left a list of chores for her to start in the nursery. And she had completed all of them.

She had thought a swim would refresh her, but the air was so humid the only cool place was under water. She slipped off her bathing cap and shook her long hair free. I wish I could have it cut, she thought. It is such a nuisance. But Dad wouldn't let her. It seemed unfair, especially since she did so much work around the place.

She liked working in the nursery. She loved the overpowering sweetness of the roses, the bitter dryness of the geraniums in the greenhouse, the acrid sharpness of the chrysanthemums. For her there was a clean beauty in the symmetry of rhododendron leaves, in the intricate design of pansy petals. She couldn't recall when she hadn't loved flowers.

She remembered the excitement when her father had come home one night five years ago and had announced to her and to her mother that he had bought a nursery.

"A nursery!" her mother had exclaimed.

"Well, it will be a nursery," her father had promised. "There are ten acres of land right on the parkway. And a little house—"

"But, Brad! The money!" Her mother was frightened.

"Kit, I went to the bank and they are going to give me a mortgage. They think it is a sure thing. Thousands of cars use the parkway every day. And week-ends! It's a perfect spot! In ten years I will have the biggest nursery in this part of the state," he boasted.

Kerry's twelve-year-old mind could scarcely encompass the new wonder. "Oh, Dad! When can we see it? Can we go to-night? Where is it? Can I—"

"Wait! Wait! Not so fast," her father laughed.

"Brad, I don't like it," her mother said soberly. "To give up a steady job and maybe it won't be a success . . ."

"Oh, Mother! Don't be silly! Daddy knows what he is doing. You don't know anything about it." Kerry remembered how impatient she had always been with her cautious, prudent mother.

"Kerry! Don't talk to your mother like that!" Her father's anger, slow to be aroused but alarming when it was, frightened her into an apology.

"I'm sorry," she mumbled.

"Kit," he said quietly, "there isn't a chance of failure, believe me. I wouldn't go into this unless I were confident." He put his arms around his wife's shoulders. "And it would mean we would have our own place, just the three of us," he reminded her.

That had convinced her mother. Ever since they had been married, her parents had lived with Grandma Kendall, in a big, old rambling house in Winston. Grandpa had died when Dad was fifteen, and, when Dad and Mother were married, Grandma had insisted they move in with her "for a year or two." They had lived there for fourteen years. Kerry's mother and her mother-in-law had not always seen eye to eye; it had been an armed truce at times. Grandma had always volunteered advice, and, when it went unheeded, she had retreated to her room with a "sick" headache. Dad had been torn between Scylla and Charybidis. Nine times out of ten he had given in to his mother.

When she heard about the nursery, Grandma had had a

week-long headache, but this time Dad had remained adamant. He was very good at that, Kerry thought ruefully. Sometimes he seemed so cold and unfeeling toward her; sometimes she wondered whether or not he really loved her, wondered whether or not her mother loved her. They always seemed so busy, so worried. It was true that they had had a rough time financially, even more so since they had started the nursery, in spite of Dad's glowing predictions. But there never even seemed to be time for the things Kerry wanted to do. There was never time for trips and vacations, or even picnics with her friends. She couldn't go with them even though she knew Dad would have given her permission. But she knew that the work she did in the nursery relieved her father; he didn't have the money yet to hire extra help. And the gang didn't think it strange that she worked for her father. Most of their fathers were farmers, so girls and boys both assisted with chores. Meg Lassiter, her best friend, even drove a tractor. Maybe that is why we are so healthy, she thought.

If I only weren't so tall, she mused. She recalled the shock when, on her twelfth birthday, she had stood up against the kitchen wall to be measured as she had since she was old enough to stand. Her father had announced, "Five feet and three inches!"

"Why, Kerry, you are as tall as I am!" her mother had said.

And now, at seventeen, she towered over her mother by four inches. Mrs. Kendall, knowing that her daughter was self-conscious about her height, often reminded her, "But, Kerry, models are tall. Only tall girls can really wear clothes well." But it didn't help. She wasn't going to be a model. Not that she hadn't thought about it; all girls did, no matter what they looked like.

Suddenly she opened her eyes wide and raised herself on her elbows. Had she been just thinking? Or dreaming? Something, an alien noise, had disturbed her. She peered across the sun-brilliant pool. It sounded as though there were people talking, down at the end of the lane. But it couldn't be. She distinctly remembered her father's putting up the "Closed Today" sign last night. They didn't have too many flowers to sell, but he had built a tiny shop on the parkway, hoping that next spring he would have enough plants to be able to hire someone full-time to take care of it.

"Kerry?" Her mother waved from the kitchen door.

"Want me, Mother?" she answered.

"Come on up," her mother said.

Kerry swung herself backward, straddled the diving board and stood up. She walked to the end of the board, bounced expertly on her toes twice, and dived into the pool. She flutter-kicked to the end and clambered up the ladder. Toweling her face, she ran across the grass and up the steps to the kitchen door.

"Do you hear someone down at the shop?" she asked, slinging the towel over the clothes line.

"That's what I called you for," her mother explained. "I want you to take this down to the parkway." She handed Kerry a thermos jug. "The county road crew is here. I think they must be spraying the weeds. They'll appreciate a drink of cold lemonade. Especially Tom," she added mischievously.

"Oh, Mother! You—you are the best!" Kerry hugged her.

"Don't! You'll get me all wet!" Mrs. Kendall laughed, only pretending to draw away.

Tom! She hadn't seen him in days, Kerry realized. He was the boy she had secretly admired for the past three years at Huron Central High. He was the boy that most of the girls had admired, and not so secretly. Tom was a senior, as was Kerry. He was varsity football captain, a basketball star, and president of Student Council. When he had come to one of Kerry's splash parties in June, he had seemed to like her a lot. During the summer he had dated her four times, had even asked her to go steady. Although she had wanted to say yes, she hesitated. It wasn't wise to seem too eager. At least that was what Meg had said. So Kerry promised to give Tom an answer by the end of the summer. She hadn't seen him after that.

She slipped a terry cloth robe over her suit, wiggled her feet into sneakers, picked up the jug and paper cups and ran down the steps to the lane.

"Why don't you ask Tom over this week-end for a picnic?" her mother called after her.

"I will! I'm going to!" she shouted over her shoulder. Mother can always tell what I am thinking! It was uncanny, she pondered, but she can.

The tall meadow grass, tinged with summer's-end brown, and the leggy golden rod reared shoulder-high on both sides of the dirt road. Wild grape vines wreathed the old gray rail fence. The sour odor of scarlet sumac that towered in profusion on either side of the lane made her wrinkle her nose. The blazing sun bored into the back of her head. Her feet sank into inches of dry, powdery dirt. She felt closed in, stifled, as though she were in some prehistoric world of giant plants. She remembered the line from *Macbeth:* "But now I am cabin'd, confined." That's how I feel, she thought, mopping her perspiring brow with the sleeve of her robe.

When she emerged from the lane, she halted abruptly. The crew was placing enormous boulders across the entrance, where their road joined the parkway! Tom and Mr. Bailey, the foreman, were using a crowbar to move the rocks close together.

"Tom! Mr. Bailey!" she cried. "What are you doing?"

Startled, they both looked up. The foreman spoke in low tones to Tom, who straightened up, dropped his crowbar and walked slowly toward Kerry, wiping his hands on his dungarees.

"Hi, Kerry," he said. "Hey! Is there lemonade in that thermos? I hope!"

"Yes, yes—there is, but—" she stammered, floundering between the excitement she always felt with Tom and the shock of seeing the road, the only access to the nursery, being closed.

"Good girl!" Tom said. "Give it here. I'm dying of thirst!"

Confused, she handed him the jug. He filled the cups for himself, Mr. Bailey, and the driver of the truck.

"Tom! What are you doing here? Why are you—"

"I'll walk you up to the house," Tom interrupted, capping the jug. "Come on. I'll explain."

"But I want to ask Mr. Bailey—"

"Look, he's embarrassed. You know how friendly he is with your father. Let me explain on the way back to the house." He took her by the elbow and steered her into the lane.

For a minute they walked in silence. Tom scuffled the dust

with his heavy brown work shoes; Kerry followed a step behind him. This is the way he likes it, she thought. Because he is such a BMOC, he likes to be the center of attention, just a step ahead. She had learned that much the few times she had dated him. But she had decided that she was willing to accept his conditions. Anything to be a part of the crowd. She hadn't been so far. Oh, she had gone to parties and dances, but she had never actually been "in."

She stopped, clutching his arm. He turned and she said, irrelevantly, "Your forehead is dirty."

He rubbed his fingers absent-mindedly across the smudge of grease on his tanned forehead, placed the thermos in the dried brown grass at the side of the road, took her hand and drew her over to the fence.

"Sit here a minute," he directed, lifting her to the top rail.

"Tom, I don't *want* to sit here a minute! I want to know what's happening! Do you realize that my father will have to close the nursery if he can't use this road?"

"I know! I know! But just listen to me. It's not my fault. Or Mr. Bailey's. We had orders."

"Orders? What kind of orders? From whom?"

"From the county seat. That's all I know," he answered with finality. "The county superintendent of highways called this morning and said that we were to close off this road and two others. They are not supposed to be access roads, and, since the highway department is going to widen the parkway, they are shutting off the roads."

"For good? But they can't!" she wailed. "What will we do?" She was on the verge of tears. All her father's plan, his hopes, his dreams, all his hard work, all for nothing! "Maybe—maybe when they finish widening the road, they might open it again?" She felt better. That was it! They would re-open it in a few months!

"No. They won't. This is permanent," Tom answered in a low voice. "The road won't be—it won't exist after today. I'm sorry."

But he didn't sound sorry. *He isn't, really,* Kerry thought. *He is just a little embarrassed. He doesn't care.*

"I—I guess I had better be getting back to the truck. It's quitting time." He slid off the fence and jogged down the road, the road that now led to nowhere. Balloons of dust soon screened him from view. He never looked back.

CHAPTER II

So that's that, thought Kerry dismally, as she heard the truck roar off down the parkway. I will never see him again. Nothing succeeds like success and nothing frightens people like failure. Tom is running away from us. We have never been a part of Downsville anyway; they have never really accepted us. Dad has been too busy to join any community organizations; Mother has never had the time either. It wasn't so much that we were newcomers, that we weren't farmers like the rest of them. It is because we don't have the money, the security that they have. It is because Dad is trying to build up a business on a shoestring, while they are sitting back smugly in the midst of their hundreds of acres and their hundreds of cows, she thought angrily.

And now it is all over. Dad will have to sell the place; he

will have to go back to working for someone else. He will hate that! And Mother! She never really believed in the nursery the first few years. Not really until last year when Dad showed her the books, the account books that, for the first time showed a sizable profit, enough to make a down payment on a new tractor and to purchase a thousand shrubs and fruit trees. Mother will never trust his judgment again.

Suddenly she was numb and cold, and her damp bathing suit felt clammy. Her sneakers seemed too small for her feet. She knew she should go back to the house and change, but she couldn't move. She felt sick. Her hands gripped the fence rail; she could feel the rough, splintery wood digging into her palms.

"Kerry?" Dimly she thought she heard her mother's voice. And what was that screeching, like the keening of a wild bird?

"Kerry!"

She looked up, dazed. Her mother was waving at her. She was taking the clothes from the line and the harsh grating of the clothesline pulley was the sound that Kerry had heard.

"I'm coming, right away," she called hoarsely.

Shall I tell her about the road, or wait until Dad comes home? Bewildered, she loosened her grip on the rail and slipped slowly to the ground. She picked up the thermos and trudged up the lane, the jug bumping against her leg.

As she reached the foot of the steps, she looked up. The brightly-colored bath towels hung from the line like rectangular petals of exotic flowers. The dazzling white of the sheets made Kerry squint. How Mom would hate to leave that clothesline!

She had often commented happily that the sunlight was on her laundry from early morning until late afternoon. How she had hated the drying yard at Grandma Kendall's, surrounded by tall, shadowy pines that brooded over the back lawn and permitted only a vagrant trickle of sunlight to glimmer through their dark canopy.

"Kerry! What on earth is the matter with you? You look as though you had seen a ghost!" Her mother stared at her. "Did Tom—is he—isn't he coming to your picnic?"

The sympathy in her mother's voice, the tiny worry furrows between her eyebrows, broke the dam. Helplessly, Kerry stood on the top step, the tears gushing down her cheeks.

"Kerry! What happened? What's the matter? Kerry!" Her mother dropped a half-folded towel into the basket and came toward her.

Flinging the thermos on the lawn, Kerry stumbled into her mother's arms. "Mom! Your clothesline! You will have to leave your clothesline!" She thought, irrevelantly, as she hid her face against the top of her mother's head, I am bigger than she is. I ought to be holding *her* in *my* arms.

"What on earth? What is this about my clothesline?"

"You—you will have to leave the clothesline? And Dad will have to sell the place! And we will have to live with—with Grandma! And the road is closed!" Kerry burst out incoherently.

"Come in and sit down and tell me what you are talking about!" her mother ordered, leading her into the kitchen. Mrs. Kendall peeled off Kerry's robe, sponged her daughter's face with cold water, and poured a glass of lemonade. "Here, sit down and drink this," she directed. "You will feel better." She sat across the table and waited for Kerry's sobs to subside.

Finally, Kerry was able to gulp down the lemonade. "Mom, it's awful! The county has closed off the road to the nursery!"

Her mother's eyes widened for a moment. "Closed the road? What for? For how long?"

"Permanently, Tom says. They are going to widen the parkway and we—we—Daddy will—" Hot tears ran down her face.

"I can't believe it," her mother answered quietly. "Stop crying. It isn't that serious. When Dad comes home, he will call Mr. Bailey and find out what's going on. Come on now. Go on up and take a shower and put on clean clothes. That will make you feel better." Mrs. Kendall got up, went to the sink, took the cleaning powder from the shelf and started scrubbing the enamel.

She had me fooled for a moment, Kerry thought. She had me convinced that she didn't think this was serious, but I know now she is really upset. She always dusts or polishes the copper-bottomed pans or scrubs the sink or stove when she is worried. I wish she wouldn't; I wish she would confide in me, talk to me. I am old enough now. Sometimes she is so aloof.

"Kerry, go up and take your shower!" Her mother's sharp voice splintered the silence between them.

That is another sign, Kerry thought, as she walked slowly up the stairs. When Mother is disturbed, her usually soft voice is brittle. She recalled the time she had raced down the lane on her bicycle, hit a bump and had catapulted over the handle bars into a pile of cinders. All the while the doctor had been extricating the miniscule pieces of coal and dirt from her arm, her mother had sat, holding Kerry's hand tightly and discussing, matter-of-factly, the new dress she was planning to make for the eighth grade dance. Only the needles in her mother's tone revealed that she was concerned.

A half hour later, fresh from the shower, in white shorts and blouse and white thong sandals, she went down to set the table for dinner.

"Let's eat out on the patio," her mother suggested. "If there's a breeze anywhere, it will be out there. And let's use paper plates and cups," she added, smiling.

"Thanks, Mom. I appreciate that tonight." Kerry always washed the dinner dishes and she had often asked why they couldn't use paper plates in the summer. Her father had finally told her he didn't like eating from cardboard, although he had relented and had agreed to their use when they had picnic suppers. But only once a week, he stipulated.

Maybe Mom was right, Kerry mused. Maybe this wasn't so serious. Maybe Tom had been mistaken. Mom wouldn't risk Dad's displeasure by not using china if she expected him to be disturbed by the closing of the lane.

When she had finished, Kerry stepped back, pleased. The pale lime cloth was a perfect setting for the clear yellow fluted plates and cups. She had picked some of the golden zinnias that bordered the patio and arranged them in a low dark green bowl as a centerpiece.

"Very pretty. Very pretty."

Startled, she turned, almost into her father's arms.

"Dad! I didn't hear you come in."

"I didn't. The truck is parked on the grass alongside of the highway. I couldn't drive in. Someone rolled a lot of boulders across our entrance. Do you know anything about it? Have any idea who did it?"

She looked up into his face. Calmer now, she felt like the strong one. She wanted to protect him. And suddenly she realized that she was doing what her mother did, both with her husband and with her daughter. Small as she was physically, Mom was the buffer between them and the world.

"Kerry? I asked you a question. Do you know anything about those rocks?" His black eyes peered at her sharply from the thin, weather-beaten face. The faint shadow of a beard accentuated the white hair that was beginning to streak the black at his temples.

"The rocks?" She vacillated, uncertain as to whether to tell him what Tom had predicted or whether to make light of it as her mother had.

"Brad?" Her mother called from the kitchen window.

"Yes, Kit?"

"Brad, if you're not too tired, would you take this bowl of salad out to the table?"

There they go again, Kerry thought, shutting me out. She was certain that her mother could have carried the bowl or could have asked Kerry to do it. But they want to talk alone. Why can't they let me in? Grandma was married when she was my age. I am an adult, too. I am good enough to help around the place, to do the work of a boy, but I am not good enough to be invited to discuss family problems. Why? Why? Why?

"Kerry, would you take the salad out?" her mother called as her father opened the screen door. "Dad wants to take his shower."

She is not fooling me, Kerry reflected. Not at all. She has told him, and they are going to pretend that nothing has happened.

She was right. Her father ate everything on his plate and never mentioned the absence of the china. After dinner he dozed in the chaise lounge while she and her mother cleared away the food and the dishes. Later he walked down to the greenhouse with her mother. Usually Kerry accompanied them, eager for the compliments her father always bestowed on her for her accomplishments. But tonight she let them go alone. She sat on the edge of the pool, idly dangling her bare feet in the water that was still warm from the sun. The brilliant orange and vermillion sunset had faded into an ominous gray. To the north the blackening sky was laced by streaks of lightning.

When her parents finally came back, her father praised her perfunctorily. Hurt, she stayed at the pool until long after dark. When they invited her to join them in their usual nightly treat, a soda of ginger ale and her mother's homemade ice cream, she refused, saying she was tired and wanted to go to bed.

She fell asleep immediately, listening to the distant drum roll of thunder.

CHAPTER III

She slept fitfully, her rest interrupted sporadically by the salvoes of thunder and the rain lashing against the windows. Just before dawn she woke. The thunder and lightning had stopped, but now a roaring gale swung the rain in torrents against the house. She groped her way to the window. When the wind parted the cataract of water, she caught a glimpse of the meadows and the nursery. The young maples bowed, with angry reluctance, before the tempest. The ash trees bent almost to the ground, revealing the silver-green undersides of their leaves, like a shy girl showing her crinoline.

Suddenly she smelled the delicious aroma of bacon and eggs. Dad and Mom must be having breakfast. I'm starved. Why didn't they call me, she wondered as she hastened down the stairs.

The bright kitchen light made her squint. Her father and mother were sitting silently at the table, drinking coffee. Neither of them noticed her.

"Hey, I'm starved! How about inviting a hungry stranger to breakfast?" she asked.

Her father glanced up, his eyes underlined with deep circles. Then he bent his head, not seeing her.

"Go back to bed, Kerry," her mother ordered quietly, not even turning to look at her.

"But, Mom, I'm—"

"Go back to bed!" Her mother turned and stared at her.

Angrily, Kerry stamped out of the room, ran upstairs and flung herself on her bed. They're shutting me away again! I know they are worried about the storm, about the damage it will do to the nursery, but they won't let *me* worry with them! WHY? WHY? WHY? She burrowed her head into the pillow and dozed off.

When she woke, the sun was shining brightly. She lay for a moment, staring up at the ceiling. Bands of lemon yellow light wavered across the white plaster. They look like reflections from water, she thought idly. Like the reflections I see on the roof of the boathouse out at the lake. Abruptly she sat up, slid across the bed and ran to the window.

It *was* a lake! The whole nursery was flooded! Hundreds of chrysanthemums, washed from their beds, dimpled and dipped as a soft breeze rippled the surface of the water. Floating gladioli, pink and salmon and white, nudged their way among the gold zinnias and saffron asters. The dripping silver tips of the blue spruce sparkled as the uprooted trees bobbed among the flowers and shrubs. Scarcely a plant stood upright. It was a shambles.

Kerry stared, unbelieving. In one night, the labor of years wiped out completely. This was the end for Dad. He might have been able to work something out, even though the road had been closed, but now all his stock had been destroyed. And some of it had not been paid for yet. Dizzy, sick at her stomach, she sat on the edge of the bed.

I ought to go down and see whether or not there is something I can do. But what? Help Dad clean up? Maybe salvage something? Salvage what? I have never felt so helpless. This is like the end of the world. A flood was the end of the world once. But we have no Noah's Ark to save us. What if the flowers, two by two, marched into the Ark? Cartoon-like images of mums and pansies and roses, drifting up a gangplank, crossed her confused mind.

"Kerry? Are you awake?" her mother called from the foot of the stairs.

"Be right down, Mom," she answered.

She wriggled into her oldest jeans and sweatshirt and hurried downstairs.

"Where are you going in that outfit?" her mother asked sharply.

"I thought Dad might need some help—"

"Dad doesn't need any help. Sit down and eat your breakfast," her mother answered curtly.

As she drank her orange juice, she stole a covert glance at her mother who was scouring pans. I wish I had some way of taking my mind off things, the way Mother does. What do they call it? Catharsis? Was that what it was? We talked about it in English class when we were reading Greek drama. Dad doesn't have any way of relieving his anxieties; he just retreats into himself, doesn't speak to anyone until he has resolved his troubles. Maybe I will be like Dad. But I'm not, now. I have to blow off steam somehow; I have to talk it out.

"Mother, what are we going to do now? Dad can't possibly retrieve anything—"

"Kerry, let's not discuss it. It's none of your—you don't have to—" her mother fumbled.

"You mean—it's none of my business. When is it going to be my business? I am seventeen years old, Mother. I am an adult and I am part of this family. I think I should be asked to share in decisions and plans and—"

"Kerry!" Her father appeared in the doorway. His boots were caked with dirt; his clothes, wet and stiff with mud. "Don't talk to your mother that way!" His voice was mechanical, as though he were repeating lines from a play.

"But, Dad! I want to help—and you and Mom won't let me! I don't understand it. You always say, both of you, that I am not to concern myself, that it's none of my affair. I don't feel as though I belong here. I don't feel as though you *want* me . . ." How do I dare talk this way, she wondered. I have always been a little afraid of Dad, afraid of arousing his anger. And I shouldn't be saying anything now. He looks so utterly defeated.

"Kerry," he began, as he slumped into a chair, "your mother and I—we have always tried to protect you from—we have always—*I* have always felt that it was my fault that . . ." His voice trailed off.

"Brad, not now," her mother interrupted. "Go upstairs and lie down. We will talk about it later." She helped him out of his wet jacket and walked him to the hall. He clumped slowly up the stairs.

Mutt and Jeff, Kerry thought wryly. She is so tiny and he is so tall. And yet, she is the stronger. He relies upon her, but he doesn't realize it. Even if he did, he wouldn't admit it.

"Kerry," her mother began, "your father wouldn't like this, but I am going to set you straight on a few things." She sat down opposite Kerry and poured a cup of coffee. She paused a minute, stirred cream into the coffee, sipped it slowly and then put the cup down deliberately. She folded her arms on the table, leaned forward and stared at her daughter.

Embarrassed, Kerry dropped her eyes. "I am sorry, Mom. I guess I was so upset, for you and Dad, I didn't think what I was saying. I was rude. I didn't mean to be."

"Yes, you were. And you picked a fine time for it, I must say. But that isn't what I am talking about. This thing that you have, that your father and I are a—a closed corporation, that we won't admit you to membership."

She knew. How? I never said anything about it until today.

"Ever since you were a little girl you have wanted to be treated as an adult. At Grandma's, when we lived with her, you used to sit at the dinner table and listen, with both ears wide open, to everything that was said. You were eager, almost desperate, to join in."

I remember, Kerry mused. And Grandma used to scold me, to tell me to go out to play. "Little pitchers have big ears," she used to tell Dad when she thought he was discussing something I shouldn't be listening to. And I used to listen all the harder.

"Perhaps it is because you are an only child, like Dad is, that we were afraid that you might—if you were aware of our problems—you might . . ." She paused and sipped her coffee.

Kerry plunged in. "I know, Mom. You were afraid that I would be like Dad was with his mother—with Grandma. Too attached to her. I know."

"You don't know. You don't really know, Kerry. But I think it is about time that you did. Dad wouldn't like my talking to you like this, so don't say anything to him about it. I just hope that you will realize, that you will be more—I was going to say—sympathetic, but that is a poor word to use about the way you should feel toward your father. I hope that you will really love him."

"But I do! I *do* love him!"

"Do you really, Kerry?"

"Yes, I do."

Her mother sighed. "We love people, really love them, in spite of their—their peculiarities. In fact, sometimes we love them *for* their faults."

That is why I wasn't sure about Tom, Kerry realized. I like him, like him a lot, but it isn't love, not really. He is fun to be with; he is exciting. But I couldn't stand living with him for the rest of my life. He is moody, selfish, and a bit snobbish.

"What are you thinking about?" her mother asked. "You

are miles away. You aren't even listening to me." She started to get up.

"But I am, Mother! I am listening! I was just thinking about what you said. I couldn't—I mean—I am not in love with Tom, not really. I could never marry him because I couldn't accept him the way he is."

"I should hope not! I should hope that you are not thinking of getting married, not at your age!" Her mother pushed her chair back abruptly and started clearing off the table.

"I didn't mean—I am not thinking of getting married right now. I just meant that I know what you are talking about— about you and Dad. And that, well, that is how you have to feel toward a person. To love someone you have to want their happiness before your own, no matter what they are like. Isn't that right?" Kerry pleaded.

"That's part of it," her mother agreed. "Here, help me with the dishes." She handed Kerry a dish towel.

"Mom, if we have to leave here and go back to Winston—"

"Not 'if', Kerry. *When* we go back to Winston," her mother interrupted. "What—when we go back?"

"Well, maybe you could—you could go back to the library for—for a little while every day. To get away from the house and housework—and from—from—" she stammered.

"What ever gave you the idea I didn't like housework?" Her mother turned and looked at her quizzically.

"No, I didn't mean that. But it has been rough for you, helping Dad build up the business, with all the other things you had to do. I should think you would be tired of it. And if Dad gets a regular job, you could work at the library, and get away from the house. I can always help more with the meals and the dishes and the laundry and the—"

"Whoa! You planning to quit school?" her mother laughed.

"No, I just thought—well, you did spend five years in college studying to be a librarian. And you only worked for a year. You told me, lots of times, how much you loved your job."

"I did."

"Mom, why didn't you go back then, when I was older? When we lived with Grandma?" Kerry folded the towel over the rack and leaned against the refrigerator.

"That is what I started to tell you when I didn't think you were paying attention to me. That is what I think you ought to know about." She wrung out the dishcloth and spread it on the drainboard. "Let's go out and sit on the patio. I'm going to take time out from all the millions of chores you seem to think I do every day," she laughed.

The hot sun that had already dried off the slate patio blazed in a cloudless, deep-blue sky. They dragged the chaise lounges into the shade of the elm tree and leaned back. Mrs. Kendall closed her eyes for a moment. She is so thin, Kerry thought. When we get back to town, I am going to help her more, she resolved.

Her mother opened her eyes, stretched her arms above her head. "This does feel good. When we get back to town, I think I will have a rest period every day." She frowned. "Dad would be upset if he could hear us talking this way. About moving back to town, just as though we had been away only the summer. It isn't as simple as that you know."

"I know, Mom."

"There will be bills to pay and the house to sell. But that isn't—it doesn't concern you."

"Mother! You promised!" Kerry sat upright, rigid.

"I'm sorry, Kerry. I have been so used to trying to—to protect you, as Dad says." She looked squarely at her daughter. "You know moving back to Winston means we will probably have to live with Grandma, for a little while, anyway."

"I know. But it won't be so bad. We have been away for a few years and Grandma has gotten used to not having us to— to—" She was afraid to say it, to put into words what she had felt all the time she was growing up.

"Say it, Kerry. To not having us to order around. That is what I wanted to explain to you. That is what has made Dad feel guilty all these years. He has been torn between us. You and me—and his mother. I got used to it, but it was hard in the beginning. In the very beginning, before we were married. Dad wanted more than anything else in the world to be a landscape architect. But she wouldn't let him go to college. It wasn't a question of money. He could have won a scholarship, but she refused to let him go. That is when she first started getting her headaches. I will never forget his face when he saw me off on the train to college that first year. He even told me to find someone else, some other boy. And I tried. I really tried. I went steady for a year with a boy. Mike, Mike Milner. He was a music major. My junior year I was pinned."

It seems strange to hear her talk of "going steady." And of being "pinned." I wonder what she was like when she was young. I never was curious before, Kerry realized.

"But then I came home that summer and Dad said he was

planning to go to night school. It might take him ten years but he was going to get his degree. I had known all along that I loved him, really loved him, but I was sure then. And I knew that he wouldn't ask me to marry him unless *he* was sure of— unless he was positive he would earn a degree. He needed that confidence."

"But he told me that he did go to college—at night—for a year. What happened? Why didn't he finish?"

"His mother couldn't stand being alone at night. I couldn't say anything. It was his decision. And I knew that I would marry him eventually, no matter what. So I said that we should get married and his mother could come to live with us. Then he told me." She was silent, her eyes blank. "She wanted us to come to live with her in the big house. I hated it! That fourteen-room monstrosity! But there was no other way. He couldn't leave her. And he wouldn't leave me. So we moved in."

"But college? Why didn't he go to college after the first year?"

"He couldn't. It was too much, working long hours for Mr. Giovanni, the landscape architect, sometimes until dark, and then rushing off to classes. He used to do homework until dawn." She sighed and stared vacantly into space.

In eighteen years she has never been really free, Kerry realized. She exchanged the burden of a mother-in-law for the burden of the nursery. Is that what marriage is? Does a woman have to give up her freedom, her real self? Does she have to submerge herself in her husband's life? Are all women Ruth? Whither thou goest I shall go? Thy people shall be my people?

"Couldn't you have gotten away for a few hours a day? Why didn't you stay at the library?" Kerry queried.

"The day before we were married Grandma informed us that no Kendall woman had ever worked for a living. That Dad would be embarrassed if I worked, because people in Winston would think that he couldn't support me. And she convinced him of that, too."

"Mom, I wish I had known," Kerry said softly. "I have been a—a brat sometimes. I wish I had known what you went through. I would have been better. At least, I would have tried."

"Oh, it hasn't been all that bad. I didn't tell you all this because I wanted sympathy. I wanted you to understand your father. He is well aware of how difficult it has been for us because of his mother, so he never wanted to involve you in our problems. He wanted you to be independent, free, the way he never was. Do you understand?"

"I do understand, Mom." She reached for her mother's hand. It felt so small, so helpless.

Mrs. Kendall squeezed her daughter's hand. "Now, if you have heard enough true confessions for one day, suppose you help me hang out the winter clothes."

"Hang out winter clothes? Today? With all this?" Kerry waved helplessly at the trees and shrubs that were piled in clumps in the meadow.

"There's nothing we can do about it until your father has had some rest and we sit down to talk about it. We made some plans this morning while you were sleeping. And when he gets up, we will talk about it. All right?" Her mother got up and walked briskly into the house.

A hurricane! A catastrophe! And Mother is going to air our

winter clothing! How does she do it? Maybe she has had so many disappointments in her life, one more, no matter how serious, doesn't mean much. Or she won't let it. I guess that is what Mr. Bricker meant in history class when he talked about being a fatalist.

CHAPTER IV

That night her mother was as good as her word. She and Mr. Kendall went over, item by item, their whole financial status, while Kerry sat by, listening intently.

"In a way, Brad," her mother said, "this storm may have been a good thing. Even though the road was closed, you might have hung on here, trying . . ."

"Hung on?" her father asked bitterly.

"You know what I mean," she answered. "We might have tried to stick it out, knowing that the business would never be successful, the way we dreamed it would be."

"I know, Kit," he said slowly. "You are right, as always."

He is giving in to her, the way he gave in to his mother. I don't know whether I like that, Kerry speculated. But then she has given her whole life to him. Marriage is a complicated affair. I guess I never thought beyond the wedding and the honeymoon.

"Dad, will you be able to go back to work for Mr. Giovanni?" Kerry wondered.

"Kerry, don't worry," he began.

"Brad!" Mrs. Kendall cautioned.

"All right, Kit. But I don't see why she has to—"

"Brad, from now on Kerry is going to be part and parcel of everything."

"Yes, Kit," he answered reluctantly. "I *can* go back to work for Mr. Giovanni, Kerry, back to Crystal Pond Nursery. Pete— Mr. Giovanni—told me when I left there that there would always be a job for me if I wanted it. I am going in to Winston to see him tomorrow."

But the solution wasn't that simple. His former employer was sympathetic. But there wasn't any work available, not until spring.

Finally, one evening a week later, her father came home jubilant. He burst into the kitchen where Kerry and her mother were preparing dinner and herded them into the living room.

"I went to see Don Jackson, the real estate man, about selling the house. Not only does he have a buyer, but he told me about a job—a good job—something that I can get my teeth into; it is a real challenge."

"What kind of a job?" Mrs. Kendall asked hesitantly.

"As superintendent for the old Sanford place."

"The old Sanford place? But I thought that was vacant. They just have a caretaker," Mrs. Kendall said.

"Not any more. Remember when the old man died, old man Sanford, his son married that English girl?"

"And they went to England to live," Mrs. Kendall added.

"That's right. Well, they're coming back and opening the place up again. I went over to see the son, Kenneth Jefferson Sanford the Second, and he offered me the job."

"But, Brad, will you really like that?" asked his wife.

"Kit, Sanford intends making the estate the showplace of the county. He showed me plans for greenhouses, gardens, the works. I can hardly wait."

He sounds happier than I have ever heard him, thought Kerry. "Dad, it sounds fabulous. Doesn't it, Mom?"

"Yes, it does," her mother answered. "If Dad really wants it."

"I do, Kit, I do! And I've only told you half," he said mysteriously. "There's more."

"More?" Kerry and her mother asked simultaneously.

"There's a house to go with it," he announced triumphantly.

"A house?" Mrs. Kendall asked doubtfully.

"Oh, it's not a new one, or very big, but it will be our own, Kit," he pointed out. "We won't have to go back to—to my mother's."

Mrs. Kendall's face relaxed; the tiny furrows between her eyebrows disappeared. That did it, Kerry thought triumphantly. She is as happy as Dad now!

"Well, come on, you two! What are we waiting for? Let's get dinner over so we can go see our new house," her mother said gaily.

A few hours later they drove up to the entrance to the Sanford estate. Massive grey stone pillars bracketed an intricately wrought iron gate through which Kerry could glimpse a long, winding gravel drive, bordered by huge maples that jostled each other up the road, spreading gloom and darkness beneath their thickly-woven branches.

"Where is the house, Dad?" Kerry asked, peering into the dusk.

"Just inside the gate," he answered. "It was the former superintendent's cottage and it hasn't been used for some years. It needs some work, so don't be disappointed," he warned.

He swung the iron gate wide and they walked up the drive.

Then Kerry saw the cottage of white stucco and brown trim, sitting demurely before a grove of pines. "Why, it's just like an English cottage, like the pictures of Shakespeare's cottage in our lit books in school!" she exclaimed.

"Let's hope the plumbing isn't as primitive as Will Shakespeare's," her mother commented wryly.

"Oh, everything is in good shape," her father hastened to reply. "Just needs a little cleaning and painting," he added as he opened the wooden gate that hung drunkenly on its hinges.

"Well, if this is any indication," her mother said, touching the gate gingerly.

"Oh, Mom, that can be fixed," Kerry insisted. "Come on, I am dying to see what it is like inside!"

"Be careful. The flagstones need re-setting," her father cautioned, pointing to the walk. The slabs of stone tilted every which way, upended by weeds and grass.

Kerry's first glimpse of the interior shocked her into silence. In the tiny foyer the dust lay thick on floor and baseboards; spider webs veiled the doorway. How will we ever fix this place up, she wondered incredulously. Another mountain for Mother to move! Every time Dad gets involved in some new project, she has to suffer. It isn't fair!

"When were you planning to start, Brad? Your job, I mean," her mother asked quietly, as she absent-mindedly traced designs in the dust that shrouded the shelf under a mirror.

"In two weeks, Kit," he replied.

"In two weeks! How can we—I don't think I can manage to clean this up in two weeks!"

"You don't have to do a thing. Mr. Sanford is bringing a crew in tomorrow to clean, paint, everything," he reassured her. "Come in and look at the house. You will love it," he promised.

And they did. Both Kerry and her mother fell in love with the little cottage. Especially with the cozy living room with its oak wainscoting, its tiny fireplace flanked by bookshelves that stretched from floor to ceiling, its wide window seats, its casement windows which opened on to a broad lawn sloping gently down to a brook that meandered into the woods.

After they had exclaimed over the compact, efficient kitchen and the dining room French doors that swung open to reveal a terrace, Mr. Kendall led them upstairs.

"This is our room, Kit. How do you like it?" he asked eagerly.

"Why, it's lovely," Mrs. Kendall admitted, standing in the center of the spacious bedroom. "The windows, Brad! Four of them! This will be so bright and airy!"

Pleased, her father took Kerry by the hand and led her down to the end of the hall. "Wait 'til you see your room!"

She opened the door. "Dad, it's beautiful!" she cried. Miniature pink rosebuds patterned the soft white wallpaper; the white enameled trim gleamed dimly in the pale rose rays of the setting sun. On one side of the room, between two casement windows, there was a built-in vanity and opposite it a small, white brick fireplace. The waxed floor, bleached white, mirrored the shadows of the maples and pines outside the windows.

"But, Brad, this room looks as though it has just been done over," her mother began.

"It has," her father laughed. "You see, Mr. Sanford had planned to use this as a guest house. He assumed that his new superintendent would be someone from town, someone who would have his own home and might not want to move here. His crew started renovations last week."

"Dad, it's perfect! I absolutely adore it! I can hardly wait 'til we move in! When can we? When, Dad?" she pleaded.

"In two weeks, when we have straightened things out," he promised. "There is a lot to do back at the nursery," he cautioned.

"I know! I know! But it will be nothing as long as we know we are coming here! Oh, I am so happy!" Kerry hugged her mother. "Aren't you, Mom?"

"I guess I am, Kerry. Just as long as you and Dad are," her mother said cautiously, walking into the hall.

"You will be, too, Kit. I promise," her father said earnestly. "This is our last move, ever."

"What is this room, Brad?" her mother called from across the hall.

"This is an extra bedroom, a spare room," he answered.

Kerry stared at her mother. I wonder whether he is thinking of inviting Grandma for visits, long visits, she thought. Mother is thinking the same thing. I can tell by the set expression on her face.

But neither of them could forsee the use to which the spare room would be put in the next year.

CHAPTER V

The next two weeks were bedlam. The most difficult choice Kerry had to make was selecting the books she wanted to take. Besides the novels of Dickens, Fielding, Eliot, Thomas Wolfe, Jane Austen, and Sallinger, she included all her volumes of poetry as well as her Marlowe, Shakespeare, Ibsen, and Shaw. On top of the last box she managed to squeeze in *Secret Garden, Little Women, Sara Crewe,* and *Little Lame Prince.* She couldn't discard those four books. They were a part of her growing-up.

Moving day finally came. Kerry and her parents rode in Old Faithful, as they called the nursery truck.

"Dad," Kerry began hesitantly, as she wriggled back and forth, trying to find a comfortable spot on the cracked leather seat through which the springs were beginning to protrude, "can't we trade Old Faithful for a car?"

"Not yet," he answered. "I will need it for my job for the next year. Mr. Sanford doesn't have a truck, but he said he would pay the expenses for this one. By next fall I might make enough on the deal to buy a small second-hand car that you could drive, Kerry. How would you like that?"

"I would love it! And I could drive it to school."

"Well, I don't know whether or not I will be able to swing a car this year so don't get your hopes up. By next fall, maybe."

"Let's not worry about it," her mother interrupted. "The school bus goes right by the cottage. Or you can drive Old Faithful to school," she added mischievously.

"Oh, Mother!" Kerry laughed. They both seem so contented, she thought. Dad seems so relieved. Maybe he only started the business because he felt he needed to prove his independence from Grandma; maybe he didn't really enjoy all the trials and tribulations. Maybe he undertook it because he wanted to give Mother and himself a life of their own, apart from Grandma. At any rate, I have never seen them like this before, as though they didn't have a care in the world.

By the week-end the new house was, in Mrs. Kendall's words, "put to rights." Sunday evening, when her father had persuaded her mother to go for an exploratory stroll on the estate, Kerry curled up on the couch in front of the fireplace. Tiny flames danced and twisted around the small applewood log. The gilt of the September setting sun splashed against the gleaming dark oak wainscoting, trickled along the polished floor and spilled in a pool on the faded wine Persian rug.

It seems as though we have always been here, Kerry thought. Already it looks lived in. The crimson draperies, the Wedgewood blue chairs, Dad's old red leather wing chair with the imprint of his head on the back—they seem to have been made for this warm, comfortable living room.

Suddenly the telephone interrupted her reverie. Who can it be, she wondered. The Sanfords are away for the weekend. Maybe it's Grandma; Dad said she might be coming over this week.

"Hello," she yawned into the telephone.

"Kerry? It's Meg."

"Meg! Hi! How did you get my number?" It was good to hear a familiar voice.

"Just asked information, silly. How are you?"

"Fine! Wonderful! Couldn't be better!"

"You sound it."

"Oh, Meg, you should see! We have the darlingest house! It is perfect! Listen! Could you come into town next weekend? Dad could come and get you. But maybe you wouldn't enjoy the trip in Old Faithful!" Kerry paused, waiting for Meg to answer. There was silence on the other end of the line. "Maybe Bert could drive you? And Tom might come, too. Then I could tell you all about Winston High. I start tomorrow."

"I—I don't think so. School starts here this week, too, and you know how frantic—how much there is to do the first weekend after school starts." Her voice was strangely chilly.

There is *never* anything to do except sit around and gab

[38]

about school and teachers and the football team, Kerry thought angrily. She is putting me off; she doesn't *want* to come. Why? Why this coolness all of a sudden? We have been best friends for three years, ever since we started as freshmen together at Huron Central High.

"How about the next week-end, Meg?"

"Well, I have sort of a—a—tentative date," she hesitated.

"Bring him along."

"It—it is with Tom!" she blurted out.

"With Tom? *My* Tom?"

"He is not exactly *your* Tom," Meg retorted sharply. "Look, Kerry, there wouldn't be any percentage in Tom's dating you. Why, he could only see you week-ends. And he couldn't take you to dances and games here in Huron," she rattled on.

"Why not? I don't exactly live in Alaska, you know. Winston is only an hour's drive."

"It wasn't *my* decision. I am just repeating what Tom said," Meg answered resentfully.

I'll bet, Kerry thought. I'll bet that you just couldn't wait until I left to get your pink lacquered talons on him! She could visualize Meg, with her soft, pale-gold hair, the limpid blue eyes, the figure just the right side of plumpness, feminine-female from the top of her head down to her size 5's. Just the kind of a girl any boy would fall for, given the right kind of encouragement. And Meg knew how to give the right kind of encouragement.

"What about Bert? Have you crossed him off your long list?" Kerry asked spitefully.

"Oh, him! He is sort of dull, compared with Tom. And besides, Tom is a big man on campus this year, the *big* man.
Football captain and—"

"I know. You don't have to recite his accomplishments to
me. Remember me? I used to go with Tom."

"Oh, Kerry," Meg said sweetly, too sweetly. "Let's not quarrel about a boy. I really would like to come to visit you, some
time later in the fall, after things are really humming at
Winston. I have never been in a big school and I imagine
there will be lots of boys—and—and things to do. Maybe we
could double-date."

"Let's wait and see. I may be too busy myself in a few weeks,
what with the swimming tests and cheerleading."

"You mean they have had pre-school tryouts and you have
made the swimming team and the cheering squad?" Meg
shrieked.

"No, but I probably won't have any trouble making either
one of them," boasted Kerry.

"Oh."

Kerry could see the small, smug mouth form the monosylla-
ble. She doesn't think I will. But I will, if it is the last thing
I do! I will show her and Tom how much I need either one
of them!

"Look, Meg, I have to hang up. I still haven't decided what
to wear tomorrow. I bought a couple of outfits and I can't make
up my mind." Why am I lying to her, Kerry wondered. I know
what I am going to wear to school tomorrow, the beige cotton
I have had for two summers.

"What did you get? New sweaters and skirts? Or what?" Meg asked eagerly.

"I really have to go. I can't talk any longer, Meg, really, I can't. Good-bye."

"Wait, Kerry. You aren't really angry, are you? About Tom? I mean, after all. He *is* here and I am here and—well, you know," she finished lamely.

"I know, Meg. And I couldn't care less. Honestly, I couldn't. I would have broken off with him eventually. After all, there will be dozens of boys—hundreds of them, actually, here at Winston. There are four hundred kids in my senior class alone and more than half of them are males. My only problem will be choosing among them. You know what a ball a new girl has in school, especially a senior. They will probably be standing in line for dates," she boasted.

"Look, Kerry, why don't we plan on the last week-end in September?" Meg asked eagerly. "You could come out Friday night and we could have a hen party. The gang would love to see you. And then I could go back with you Saturday to the Winston football game. If you are a cheerleader, you will— you could probably get me a date with half the football team, couldn't you?" she wheedled.

Visions of all those fullbacks and tackles are dancing in her shrewd little head, Kerry thought. She wants her cake and she wants to eat it, too. She wants Tom and she wants the chance to meet boys here, too.

"I better wait and see. I will let you know."

"O.K. I'll 'phone you and—"

"No, don't call me. I'll call you," Kerry snapped. She slammed down the telephone and flung herself on the couch. The fire had burned to cold ashes; the dark shadows of the September evening shrouded the room. It suits my mood, she thought ruefully. A little while ago I was happy; now I feel like the tag end of a gloomy, rain-soaked day. And just because my best friend snagged my boy friend. Grow up, girl. There are hundreds of males at Winston High. You just told Meg so.

But 'way down deep, she knew she was only whistling in the dark. Sure, there were boys to spare at the new school, but there was no guarantee that they would like her. Just any boy wouldn't do. He had to be special, extra special, just to show Meg. And to show Tom, to show him what he had missed. That was the important thing. She visualized herself, strolling casually into a dance at Huron High, on the arm of a tall, handsome boy. Tall! He had to be tall, she thought unhappily. How many times she had refused even to dance with a boy shorter than she. And so many of them were.

"What are you doing in the dark?" Her mother's voice startled her. She had been so wrapped up in her thoughts that she had not heard them come in.

"Why so glum?" her father asked, snapping on the light. "You let the fire go out," he chided, kneeling down to start a fresh one.

Kerry stared silently as the wood chips flared and the flames crackled around the logs.

"Kerry, is something wrong?" her mother asked as she shrugged off her jacket.

"No. Nothing—really," Kerry hesitated.

"There is. When we left, you were sitting here on the couch with a broad smile on your face," her mother replied.

"Oh, it's just that—that—Meg called," Kerry began.

"And that is the cause for your long, long face?" her mother asked.

"Oh, Mom! She is going with Tom!"

"So that's all it is," her mother said, sitting next to her. "Didn't you expect it? That he would date other girls?"

"But he could have waited," Kerry faltered. "He could have waited!"

"You mean . . . 'the funeral baked meats did coldly furnish forth the marriage tables'?"

"Oh, Mother," she wailed. "Quoting *Hamlet* at a time like this!"

"I'm sorry," Mrs. Kendall said softly, putting her arm around her daughter and drawing her close. "I shouldn't have been so facetious. But it isn't so serious as all that. You told me yourself that you weren't really—that you never thought seriously about Tom, that you never thought of marrying him."

"I should say not!" her father interrupted, getting up from the hearth. "Marriage? At your age?"

"Dad, how about your getting you and me a cup of coffee?" Mrs. Kendall asked.

"I know. I can take a hint," he laughed, as he disappeared into the kitchen. "You two want to talk."

"Kerry," her mother began, "this seems like a catastrophe to you right now. It isn't, really."

"But, Mother, I really like Tom!"

"Of course you do, more so because he was the first boy you ever really liked. Remember the dates you used to have? When you first started going out with boys? I would ask you what had happened to Jack or Eddie or Arthur or Dick. And you would say, 'That goon!' You never wanted to go steady until you met Tom. You know, they say that you never really forget your first love, that actually you are in love with love the first time. And maybe, probably, even if you *had* gone steady with Tom, you would have met someone else here at Winston High that you would like just as much. Then you would have struggled with your conscience, asking yourself how you could tell Tom that you wanted to break off with him."

She is right, as usual, Kerry realized. Perhaps that was why Tom was so exciting to be with. I had never really enjoyed a boy's company before. I just liked being with him. He was glitter and glamour, starlight and moonlight.

And then a tiny thought wriggled through her mind. Was he exciting because he was a BMOC? Was I flattered that he wanted me to be his girl? Slowly she admitted that Tom's attraction had been, in some measure, his status at Huron High.

"Mom," she began slowly, "I guess you are right. I was just thinking. Maybe I was—well, sort of impressed with Tom. That's why I was so 'gone' on him."

"Maybe. Maybe. At any rate, tomorrow is the big day. You will have so much to do and so much to think about, once you are officially a Winston High senior, you won't have time to think about old flames, no matter how brightly they once burned. Now," her mother said briskly, "why don't you go out and get a cup of hot chocolate, bring it in and Dad will tell you about his plans for the formal garden. He is going to let you help with the design."

"Coming up! One cup of hot chocolate," her father announced as he came in from the kitchen. He set the tray on the coffee table. "You see, I already anticipated your desires, madame," he smiled, handing Kerry the cup. "And I fixed some sandwiches, real French cuisine," he joked. "What will it be? Peanut butter and jelly? Or jelly and peanut butter?"

Later, warm inside and out, Kerry was nodding sleepily as she listened to her father outline his project.

"Come on, I think it is about time we all went to bed," her mother said, shaking her gently.

Kerry got up, said good-night, and stumbled sleepily up the stairs. She dreamed that she was leading the student body in a cheer and the whole student body was made up of couples, couples whose faces were Tom's and Meg's.

CHAPTER VI

Kerry woke early the next day. She lay, wide awake, gazing contentedly around the room. It was perfect, soft, feminine, yet adult. The maple twin beds with their snow-white candlewick spreads, the oval pink and gray hooked rug splashed with roses, the maple desk and dainty Windsor chair—somehow, despite the fact that she had lived with them for several years, they looked new and beautiful in this room. She glanced at the green boudoir chair and footstool to match that sat in front of the fireplace. Her mother had found them in Grandma's attic, and, over the elder Mrs. Kendall's protests, had re-covered them. That was one time Mom had her way, Kerry thought triumphantly.

She looked at the other bed. She had had twin beds ever since she was five years old. She recalled that she had always thought that the other bed was for a sister. Once, when she was eight and she had been helping her mother dust, she had suddenly looked up as she was polishing the headboard and asked, "Mother, am I ever going to have a baby sister? It seems like a waste, having an extra bed and nobody in it."

"Some day, Kerry," her mother laughed, "some day."

But "some day" had never come. Why, she never knew. Perhaps it was because they had lived with Grandma; perhaps she would not have tolerated another grandchild under foot. I am going to have half a dozen children, Kerry decided as she kicked off the covers and slid into her scuffs. Three girls and three boys. She shivered in the early September chill so she took a quilted robe from the closet and hurried down to the warmth of the kitchen.

By 7:45 she was ready for school. She pirouetted in front of the mirror to see that she looked just right. The beige dress accented her bronzed skin and deepened the topaz of her eyes. She had decided to coil her long, taffy, sun-bleached hair on top of her head for the first day. It makes me look taller, she realized ruefully. But, let's face it; I *am* tall. Last summer she had tried to explain to her mother that she wouldn't look so gawky if her parents would let her have her hair cut. Besides, it was such a nuisance; it took ages to shampoo and dry.

"Your father likes it, Kerry. He wouldn't want you to have it cut," her mother said with finality.

And that is because Grandma has always said that a woman's beauty is in her hair, long hair. That is why you never cut yours, Mother, she thought. As long as Kerry could remember, her mother had worn hers in the same style, simply pulled straight back and wound in a bun, clinging low on the neck. Kerry had often, when she was a child, brushed and combed her mother's long brown hair. Her mother would lean back, relaxed, and close her eyes, half dozing. I ought to do that now, once in a while, Kerry thought. She would like it.

"Kerry? Are you ready?" her mother called.

"All ready, Mom. I'll be right down," she answered, sliding a white bracelet up her tanned arm. I wonder if my shoes are too summery, she mused as she contemplated her white thong sandals. I don't know what they wear in a big school like Winston. Well, it's too late to change now, she decided as she ran down the stairs.

"Want me to drive you to school?" her father asked.

"No, thanks, Dad. Not in Old Faithful."

"I just thought that—the first morning—"

"She can take the school bus, Brad. It stops right outside our gate. That way she will get a chance to meet some of her classmates," Mrs. Kendall said.

When she climbed on the bus, Kerry saw how wrong her mother was. There wasn't a boy or girl over fourteen, it seemed. Feeling a bit out of place, she sat in the first empty seat.

Old Faithful would be better than this, she thought ruefully, listening to the din in the back of the bus. Lanky, half-grown boys drummed a tatoo on the windows; chubby girls shrieked and squealed in delight.

"You, too?" a voice whispered in her ear.

She turned to face the girl in the seat behind her. Coal-black eyelashes swept the plump cheeks; black eyebrow pencil described a perfect arc above brown eyes that swam in a pool of green eyeshadow; her hair was a pyramid of glittering brass waves that crested almost a foot above her brow.

"Won't 'they' let you drive, either?" the girl persisted. Kerry could hear the quotation marks in her voice.

"They?"

"Mm. Your parents. Mine won't. Until I am eighteen! Next year!"

She doesn't look seventeen. Kerry was surprised.

"It isn't exactly that. I mean, I drive," Kerry said.

"And you ride this crumby old bus with all these monsters? You must be out of your mind!"

"Well, we don't have our new car yet, and I wouldn't want to take the one we have to school." I can't tell her we have only a truck.

"Forget it, chum. The older the better. Unless you belong to the inner circle—the Crew."

"The Crew?"

"Crew—with a capital C! The gals and guys that run the school, and don't you forget it. That is THE crowd, THE wheels, at good ol' Winston High. You'd better believe it! But, say, what is your name? I am Andrea Stark. Move over, monster, and let me out," she said to the twelve-year-old who was sharing her seat. She slid in next to Kerry.

"I am Kerry—Kerry Kendall."

"Hey, that's some name. Sounds like a movie star. Is it for real?" She burbled on, not waiting for an answer. "Listen, you don't rate unless you have a car at school. Even if you don't belong to the Crew, you just have to have a car."

Kerry was silent. This wasn't like Huron Central. There

practically everybody took the bus. And there wasn't any Crew, either. Or was there?

Andrea babbled on, filling Kerry in on who was who at Winston. She strung names haphazardly like a rope of colored lights, each one brighter and more important than the previous one. Kerry was dazzled, confused, and speechless. She was glad when the bus finally swung into the school parking lot.

Hundreds of cars were nosed into the curb behind the huge brick building. As Kerry and Andrea stepped down from the bus, a red convertible, decorated with flames on doors and hood, spun around the bus, just missing the two girls.

"Hey, you jerky kid! Watch where you're goin!" the bus driver roared angrily.

The driver, a slim, dark boy with a fixed sneer on his angular face, hooted derisively and revved up his motor as he cramped his car into a parking space.

"Who is that?" Kerry asked as they crossed to the sidewalk that skirted the football field and wound toward the high school.

"Duke Kraft. Douglas Underwood Kraft. D-U-K. Duke. Get it?"

"And is he one of the Crew?"

"You'd better believe it! He IS the Crew. Or, at least, he hopes to be."

"What do you mean?"

"Well, every year a senior boy sort of heads the Crew."

"You mean they have elections? Like a club?"

"More like a fraternity or a sorority. Oh, it's unofficial; the school doesn't recognize it. Bull knows it's in existence, but he pretends he doesn't. Bull is the warden, the principal, Mr. Durham. He looks the other way until they pull some real wild stunt. Then he calls them into his office and gives them a lecture. Off the record, you understand. He doesn't dare do anything else. Their parents pull too much weight in this town."

"They sound as though they run the school and the town, too. I don't understand. How do they get away with—"

"You will, chum. You will," Andrea interrupted. "Come on, I'll take you to the guidance office to get your schedule. Do you have any idea what classes you will be in?"

"No. All I know is they told me that I could register by mail, because we were moving. And they had to get my records from my old school."

"You're lucky. You won't have to wait in line."

They didn't. In five minutes, they were both walking down the corridor.

"Let's see the mournful news, chum," said Andrea, snatching Kerry's schedule card. "Hey! You must be in the top group!" she shrieked.

"Top group?" Kerry was bewildered.

"Mm. We are homogenized here."

"Homogenized!"

"That's what we call it. The kids, I mean. The intellectual cream on top," she sneered. "Homogeneous grouping the guidance department calls it. They give you all kinds of tests when you first come into High and then group you according to the results. Like a card from an IBM machine," Andrea said scornfully. "And the academic group you are in determines the social group you are in. Or maybe it is the other way around."

"Are you—what group are you in?" Kerry asked hesitantly.

"Oh, I am in part of the cream," Andrea answered. "At the bottom, though. Just above the skim milk."

Kerry was perplexed and a little distraught. I don't think I am going to like this place. It wasn't like this at Huron; everybody was mixed up with everybody else. Everybody knew everybody else. There weren't these social strata or academic strata, either.

"Don't look so glum!" Andrea laughed. "It isn't all that bad. You will survive; we all do. Lots of kids get lost in the shuffle, but they survive. The skim milk curdles once in a while and the kids get into trouble or just up and leave school. They can't take the—the undemocratic system we have here," she explained, pushing her way through the crush of students that were milling about in the hall. "Hey!" she screamed, as she looked closely at Kerry's card. "You are in my homeroom! I guess the machine broke down. Usually we are alphabetized. You know, all the A's, B's, C's in one homeroom. Probably there was an empty seat in Room 30. That is where I register— with the R's, S's, and T's."

When they reached Room 30, Andrea led Kerry to a back seat, cautioned her to save one for her, and circulated about the room, renewing old friendships. They all seemed to like Kerry's new friend. All except a group of four, two girls and two boys who sat at the front of the room. They only nodded perfunctorily at Andrea and then turned to talk among themselves.

"Who are they?" asked Kerry when the other girl had finished her tour of greetings.

"That, my friend, is part of the Crew," she explained. "That tall, dark one is Merry, spelled M-E-R-R-Y. Merry Raleigh. She is a model."

"A model?" Kerry started.

"Mm. She used to work every afternoon. Had her schedule arranged so she could leave at noon to go into the city."

She doesn't look so merry to me, Kerry decided. The girl, whose thin scarlet lips seemed to be set in a perpetual grimace, suddenly saw Kerry. She bent over and whispered something to the other three, who, in turn, glanced over their shoulders. They all laughed, disdainfully, Kerry imagined. Am I going to be shut out here, too, she wondered unhappily. Just when I have convinced my parents to accept me as an adult, am I going to be excluded in school? I can't. I won't. I will have to get into that inner circle!

"The other girl is Tracey Shaffer," Andrea continued. Tracey was red-haired, green-eyed, aristocratic. "The boys are Ted Torrance, Tiger, they call him. And Bob Ramsey." The boys, both blondes, wore almost identical clothes, Madras jackets and beige gabardine slacks.

"Everybody is so dressed up," Kerry commented, glancing at Andrea's white silk jersey dress, belted in gold.

"Oh, we always dress up for an assembly," Andrea explained, touching her gold earrings. "We have one once a week. And we have one today, always on the first day."

"Do the girls always wear heels?" Kerry asked, looking at Andrea's white spikes.

"Mm. And stockings. And the boys have to wear white shirts, jackets and ties."

"But those boys—Tiger and Bob—are wearing tan shirts."

"They are the Crew. I told you. They don't conform, except to wear jackets and ties."

"I think it is silly," Kerry commented. "It sounds like—like a fashion parade! It must be expensive!"

"It is. And you don't mention money. It just isn't done. Don't let anyone else hear you say that," Andrea warned. "Conform, chum. Conform, or you won't be 'in.' Wait until you get into the Crew. Then you can be a non-conformist," she advised. "Amos says they are more conformist than anyone else. He says that they conform to non-conformity. Sound confusing?"

"Yes. Who is Amos? And what do you mean when I get into the Crew? I don't think I have a chance and, if I did, I don't know whether or not I would want to, not after what you just told me."

"First, Amos is my father. Dr. Amos Stark, psychiatrist, skier, tennis player, and part-time father," she said bitterly.

Just then there was a lull in the chatter. Kerry looked up. A slim, trim, white-haired woman appeared in the doorway and stood quietly watching the class.

"That is Grierson, our homeroom teacher," Andrea whispered. "She is ancient. Must be fifty if she is a day. But what a teacher! She has the top senior English classes. You will have her. I will, too, second period."

"That is when I have English," Kerry said happily. "We will be in the same class."

"I hope you like English," Andrea said. " 'Cause if you

don't, you will sweat in Grierson's class. She really makes you work."

"It is my second favorite subject," answered Kerry. "Next to botany."

"Botany! You don't mean it!" Andrea was incredulous.

"I am going to be a—I want to go into horticulture," Kerry explained hesitantly.

"Horticulture? You mean flowers and trees and all that jazz?"

"Why not?" Kerry asked defiantly.

"For a girl? That's real kookie."

"I don't think so. My father is—is—sort of a horticulturist."

"What do you mean? Sort of?"

"Well, we had our own nursery, but now he is the superintendent for Mr. Sanford."

"Not for Kenneth Jefferson Sanford the Second!" Andrea squealed. "You lucky, lucky girl!"

"Why am I lucky?" whispered Kerry.

"Haven't you seen Kenneth Jefferson Sanford the Third?"

"No. Should I? Who is he?"

"Only a dream. The dreamiest! He is a senior this year! He just came back to town this summer. And right away, he was adopted by the Crew. He went to a couple of prep schools and got bounced from a couple, too, I hear. Everybody thinks that is why his father decided to come back to Winston—to give the prodigal son some roots, as Amos says." She paused, staring in awe at Kerry. "And you are going to be living right there—a couple of hundred yards from the smoothest boy this old town has ever seen!"

The bell interrupted her. Mrs. Grierson closed the door, rapped gently on the desk and the class was silent. Quietly but firmly she delivered instructions for the day. She is very sure of herself, Kerry reflected. Even those four up front are listening to her respectfully.

As the teacher finished calling the roll, the door opened and a boy sauntered in. Miss Grierson glanced at him coldly and directed him to a seat. He strolled slowly down the aisle and slumped behind his desk.

"That's him! That's Kenny Sanford!" hissed Andrea. "Isn't he a dreamboat?" she drooled.

He *is* good-looking, admitted Kerry. His face was deeply tanned; his brown hair, crew cut, bristled blonde at the temples. He was a symphony in brown and beige—chocolate brown slacks, a camel's hair jacket, beige shirt, brown tie and beige bucks. I'll bet his eyes are brown, too, to match, Kerry thought. I am sure that he would never permit his eyes to be any other color. At that moment, he turned languidly and his eyes—they *were* brown—swept arrogantly over the class. They didn't pause; they didn't seem to see anyone, not even the quartet in the front seats.

That is that, Kerry my girl, she thought. For a moment she had hoped. She had wanted this boy, this dreamboat, to look at *her,* to notice *her.*

"He is reconnoitering," Andrea whispered.

"Obviously the females in Room 30 aren't included in his campaign," Kerry answered, as the bell for assembly rang.

CHAPTER VII

At nine o'clock the entire student body met in the auditorium. This is a lot different from Huron, Kerry realized, gazing in awe at the spacious stage with its navy blue velvet curtain beneath a proscenium decorated with scenes from Shakespearean plays. Navy draperies were drawn over tall windows at the sides, and overhead brilliant chandeliers blazed. The cacophony of a hundred-piece school orchestra drowned out even Andrea's high squeals as she chattered in Kerry's ear.

Since they were seniors, Room 30 sat at the front of the auditorium. Sitting in the row of eight chairs lined up on the stage were Merry, Tracey, and Duke. There were three other students and a man who looked like a teacher.

"What are they doing on the stage? The Crew, I mean," shouted Kerry over the din.

"I told you. They snag all the offices in the school. Duke is student council prez, Tracey is senior prexy, and Merry is head of the Leaders Club. That boy on the left, the big oaf, is Neal Maxon, captain of varsity football. The one next to him is Turk Janis, president of the Varsity Club. All the athletes, the muscle men with bird brains, belong to that," Andrew rattled on.

"Who is that other boy?" Andrea asked, pointing to a lean, black-haired student who sat—it seemed brooded—a little apart from the others.

"Oh, him? That's Mark Lee," she answered curtly, offering no other explanation.

"But who is he?"

"He's 'way out, chum. He actually turned down an invitation to join the Crew."

"Why? Then what is he doing sitting up there with the other—"

"He is Runes prexy."

"Runes?"

"That is the club that does the year book, the school paper, and the literary magazine. And we—they—write publicity for the *Winston Star,* the local gossip sheet, the town newspaper."

"We? Did you say 'we'? Are you a member of the Runes?"

"Mm, but I don't brag about it."

"Why not? Are you ashamed or what?"

"It's not that," Andrea hesitated. "It's just that—well, it's not the thing to do—here—in this school."

"Honestly, Andrea! You say you are a good English student, and you must be able to write. You must like to write or you wouldn't have joined—"

"Look, chum. It was the only thing left. I am no athlete. I don't dig music or art particularly. And I am certainly not going to join the Drama Club and flit around the stage. So I joined the Runes. You have to do *something!* You have to be a part of *something* in high school!"

She is right, Kerry agreed. It isn't any fun being a loner, either in your family or at school. And what if it does mean conforming? Following the crowd? It is better than wandering on the fringes and wanting "in."

The orchestra concluded its march with a deafening flourish, and Duke stepped to the center of the stage. Immediately the auditorium rocked with applause. He smiled faintly, almost arrogantly, held up his hands for silence and led the Pledge of Allegiance and the prayer. After the singing of the "Star-Spangled Banner," he presented Mr. Durham, the principal.

The principal lumbered to the rostrum. He was the biggest man Kerry had ever seen. He was over six feet, four inches tall and on the verge of being obese.

"He is enormous!" Kerry whispered.

"He weighs three hundred pounds, and it's mostly beef! He played center for State; they called him 'Bull' in college. We do, too—Bull Durham," she giggled.

His huge hands gripped the rostrum and there was dead silence as he leaned over to peer at the audience. "This is a new school year!" he boomed. "And I want you all to turn over a new leaf! You're here to study! And don't you forget it! We will have no nonsense, no fooling around! Or out! O-U-T! Out!" he jerked his fat thumb over his broad shoulder. "Now we're going to hear from the officers of the clubs in the school." The students clapped wildly, stamped their feet, and whistled piercingly as he rolled back to his chair.

That is the shortest and most peculiar speech I have ever heard a principal deliver, Kerry pondered. He sounds as though he *wants* the students to misbehave so that he can punish them. She recalled the initial assemblies at Huron High. Mr. Driscoll, a short, balding, nervous man, had always talked interminably about scholars and College Boards and ideals. No one had ever really listened, even though they sat in respectful silence. But this school certainly listened to Mr. Durham!

Each of the presidents made a brief speech of welcome; each was followed by thunderous applause. Except for Mark Lee's. There was only a perfunctory patter when he finished.

"What is the matter! Don't the kids like him?" asked Kerry.

"I told you! He refused to join the Crew!"

"But what has that got to do with the way the rest of the school feels? Don't they resent the Crew? I should think they would be glad that Mark—"

"You are naïve! Even though you don't belong here at Winston, you still hope. Every kid in this auditorium hopes he will make it, hopes he will be one of the 'ins.'"

She is right, Kerry thought. But before she could answer, the orchestra struck up a march and the students rose to file out of the assembly. As they walked along the corridor, Kerry could hear loud talking and occasionally an uproar from most of the rooms, but, when they reached her homeroom there was merely a quiet hum of conversation. I guess kids know what is expected of them, Kerry thought. If parents and teachers expect us to be juvenile delinquents, we will; if they expect us to behave and let us know that, we will. At least that is the way it seems. My homeroom knows what Mrs. Grierson wants; ergo, they don't act up.

The rest of the day was a blur, a kaleidoscope of classes and corridors and hundreds of new faces. In addition to English, Kerry and Andrea also had the same gym class and the same lunch period. They both lingered too long in the girls' room after lunch so Kerry had to hurry to her next class which was botany. It was on the top floor and she had difficulty trying to hurl herself through the crowds that jammed the halls. She slid into her seat, breathless, just as the bell rang for the beginning of the period.

The botany room was a lecture room; the seats were graduated in tiers. Through the opaque skylight the afternoon sun cast a milky glow over the faces of the students. Immediately over Kerry's head there was a single clear glass pane and the bright sunlight, pouring down on the white pages of her notebook, made her squint.

The instructor was a tall, sandy-haired young man who looked more like a high school senior than a high school teacher. Although the other male instructors still wore their jackets and ties, the botany teacher sat slouched on a stool, minus his coat with his collar unbuttoned, and his sleeves rolled up.

"Ladies and gentlemen," he began, "this is not the greenhouse, despite the heat from above." He pointed to the sky-light and the class laughed hesitantly.

"As you know, if you read the local paper, the science department has ordered shades for this room. When they will arrive is anybody's guess. Meanwhile we will suffer in silence—and sweat. And the young lady in the first seat," he continued, indicating Kerry, "will be able to continue her sunbaths every afternoon and retain that very becoming tan."

Every head turned toward Kerry. The bright sunlight beamed down on her like a spotlight. She could feel a blush rising from her neck to her ears. A couple of boys whistled softly, in obvious admiration. Kenny Sanford just looked, but he looked carefully.

I don't like the way he is looking at me, Kerry thought angrily. She stared back at him, but she was the first to drop her eyes.

"Gentlemen," the teacher jested, "this is *not* an anatomy class. Shall we turn our attention to *this* specimen at the front of the room? To yours truly, Doctor Rufus Sherry?" He pointed to himself. The class roared.

Kerry was horrified. She had never been so embarrassed in her life. Did he think he was going to establish rapport with the class by poking fun at her? I don't like him. How will I ever stick it out for a whole year! And my favorite class, too!

"As most of you know, Miss Wynn, my predecessor in this hot-house, has left for greener pastures. No pun intended." He waited for the laughter. After it had subsided, he continued, "That will probably be the last time you will ever laugh in this class." The students glanced at each other, puzzled. "I mean," he went on, "this is a rough course, the way I teach it. I like teaching and I like teaching botany more than anything else in the world. Otherwise I wouldn't be here." He paused. The class was motionless, listening intently. "I expect you, there- fore, to work like slaves, to do every assignment, completely and perfectly. And the only A's given—I should say earned—will be earned by those people who do more than they are assigned, who do work over and above and beyond the call of duty. Any questions?"

A boy in the top row of seats raised his hand. "Dr. Sherry, does anyone else teach botany?" The class snickered.

"Not that I know of. But if you would like to leave now and have your schedule changed to physics or chemistry, you may go." The teacher didn't seem annoyed; he was making a simple statement. "If you are taking this course only to get credits, you had better leave now." No one moved. "Maybe I had better ask you why you are in here. Suppose you stand up, give your full name and the reason why you signed up for botany."

The class groaned but they obeyed. Most of them are giving false reasons, Kerry thought, as she listened. Half of the class assured Dr. Sherry that they had always been interested in the subject and wanted to know more about it; some of the girls said they expected to have homes and gardens of their own some day and therefore wanted to learn about flowers and shrubs and trees.

When it came Kenneth's turn, he rose languidly and an- nounced arrogantly, "Kenneth Jefferson Sanford the Third. I am taking botany because I heard it was a snap course with Miss Wynn and I have no intention of sweating over chem or physics." He slouched back into his seat and stared defiantly at the instructor. There was a nervous silence. Obviously the students were unaccustomed to such bravado.

"Well, Kenneth Jefferson Sanford the Third, you at least are honest," Dr. Sherry replied, his eyes sweeping the class. "I like that. But it takes more than honesty to pass my course. Think it over. If you have the guts, if you think you can take it, come back tomorrow. Next?" He passed on to the next student in that row.

It was Mark Lee. As he stood up, there were a few snickers. Oblivious, he said, seriously, "I am Mark Lee and I am taking botany because I think it will help me to be a better writer." His voice was deep; his speech unusually articulate. "I think, in order to be a good writer, you have to know, to learn just about everything about everything. Botany is one field in which I am completely ignorant."

What a beautiful voice, Kerry thought. And he isn't the least embarrassed. It must be difficult to be in his position, to be the one who is out of step. He sounds so sure of himself. Maybe that is why he didn't join the Crew. He doesn't need them. But I do; I need them. I *have* to belong; I cannot stand alone the way Mark does.

When it was her turn, Kerry stood up and said, in a low voice that barely carried to the front of the room, "I am Kerry Kendall and I am taking botany because I am going to be a horticulturist." She sat down quickly.

Dr. Sherry's eyes widened. Kerry could tell he was pleased. "A very worthy goal, Kerry," he said. "But an ambitious one, especially for a girl. You may change your mind before the year is over."

"I don't think so, Dr. Sherry. I know it is hard work. I have had practical experience in my father's nursery for a couple of years."

Every head swiveled toward her, for a second time that period. Mark nodded approvingly and smiled at her. Even Kenneth deigned to glance at her.

"Good girl!" the teacher commented. "And now, ladies and gentlemen, your assignment for tomorrow."

"Assignment! For tomorrow!" The class groaned as one. One bolder boy said, "Not the first night, Doc! Not for tomorrow!"

"Tomorrow and tomorrow and tomorrow," Dr. Sherry went on relentlessly. "Tonight I should like you to read and be able to discuss the introductory chapter in your text. Next week I shall give you a reading list. I will expect you to read, outside of class, a dozen or more books that I think are good background material. They are not textbooks. Texts are just skeletons. We are going to spend most of our time studying the flesh."

Before he could say any more, the bell rang and the class, muttering and complaining, hurried out.

"Kerry," Dr. Sherry called as she started for the door. "Could I see you a moment?"

"Well, I have study hall next period on the first floor and I don't know whether I will have time to make it."

"I will give you a pass to study hall," he interrupted. "Did you really mean it? About being a horticulturist? But, of course you did," he answered himself. "Look, if you would like to do extra work—if there is anything I can do to help you?"

"First, by not embarrassing me in class!" Kerry blurted out without thinking.

Dr. Sherry roared with laughter. "Another honest student! Like that Kenneth What's-His-Name-the-Third!" Soberly he continued, "I am sorry. I apologize. It is my first teaching job and I vowed I wouldn't be like the sourpusses, the hatchet-face teachers I had in high school. I guess I do have a tendency to be a bit facetious at times, too. Got called down in high school and in college lots of times for it. I promise I won't make you uncomfortable again. O.K.?"

Kerry was more embarrassed than ever. A teacher has never confided in her nor had she ever heard one apologize before. Most of them act as though they had drunk from the original fountain of knowledge, she thought; most of them would never admit they were wrong.

"O.K.," she answered shyly.

The bell rang as the teacher signed a late pass for her and she hurried down to the study hall.

On the school bus that afternoon she related the incident to Andrea. The other girl simply commented, "Yes, I heard all about it. Don't apple-polish. Not if you want to get into the Crew. They don't like it."

At dinner that evening she reviewed the whole day for her parents. When she told her father about the "greener pastures" pun, he said wryly, "It's a wonder he didn't say you had a tough row to hoe when you told him you wanted to be a horticulturist."

"Oh, Dad! That's not funny!" she scolded.

Then all three of them dissolved in laughter.

As she bent over her homework that night, Kerry's thoughts wandered back to school and she went back over each minute of her first day at Winston High. It was confusing, she decided, but I like it. I like it better than Huron High. I can hardly wait to tell Meg!

And then a tiny sliver of doubt stabbed at her. What about the Crew? Will I make it? Will they accept me? I *have* to! Then, for some strange reason, Mark Lee's face was superimposed on her botany textbook.

CHAPTER VIII

During the next few weeks Kerry felt as though she were riding on a merry-go-round. Each day the same room, the same class and the same teacher would appear momentarily; then she would swing past them dizzily until the next day. She never missed the slow, leisurely pace of her old school, however; she enjoyed the pressure at Winston.

Her father and mother seemed to thrive on their new life, too. There were no more long week-end trips to the mountains for Mr. Kendall; he was at home each evening for dinner. Kerry found herself listening happily for the sound of Old Faithful chugging down the drive from the main house, for the syncopation of the ancient engine with its one-two-pause, one-two-pause. At night, while she was doing her homework at her desk, she could hear the faint hum of conversation from the living room, conversation punctuated often by laughter. She couldn't remember when there had been such an aura of happiness in their home.

Each night she brought home some incident, some academic success which she placed like an offering before her parents. She made the swimming team; she was elected homeroom secretary, as a result of Andrea's electioneering. When Mrs. Grierson returned the first compositions, she asked Kerry to remain after class and suggested that she try out for *Winston Courier,* the school paper, and for the *Tatler,* the school yearbook. Kerry hesitated at signing up for the two activities because she was afraid it might jeopardize her chances of being asked to join the Crew. Finally she decided to try out for the cheering squad first; Andrea had informed her that making it would almost automatically mean an invitation to join the "right" crowd.

For two weeks before try-outs she practiced every noon in the gym along with a dozen or more other hopefuls. Since Andrea was familiar with the cheers, she coached Kerry. She even promised that her father would pick them up after the finals, since the school bus left promptly after dismissal.

When the day finally arrived, Andrea had to see Mark about an article for the *Courier* so she told Kerry that she would meet her in the girls' room after she had received her assignment. While Kerry waited, she nervously applied lipstick for the fifth time and looked at herself anxiously in the full-length mirror at the rear of the girls' room. On the other side of the partition, she could hear voices, the voices of the varsity cheerleaders, all of whom, Andrea had told her emphatically, were members of the Crew. They were to judge the try-outs.

"Who all are trying out?" she heard one girl ask.

"You know them all. Babs Russell, Tina Crowell. Here, see for yourself. Here's the list." That was Tracey Shaffer's voice. Tracey was the captain of the squad.

"Who is this? Kerry Kendall? I don't know any Kerry Kendall," one girl said.

"That new girl. She is a senior," answered Tracey.

"Do we want her, Tracey?" another voice asked.

"She is too tall," Tracey answered abruptly.

Kerry froze. Too tall? What did that have to do with it?

"Have you told Coach that we don't want her?" a girl queried.

"Coach agrees," Tracey continued. "She says that looks are as important as performance. You know that is the reason why we always win the county cheer-leading championships. We look good! We look like a chorus line; everybody is about the same height and weight. We all wear our hair the same way, too!"

Kerry's hands flew to her head. Oh, why didn't I have my hair cut! I look like somebody out of the Gay Nineties!

"But, Tracey, if she is the girl in my botany class, she is a knock-out! It *is* the same one. I remember. Kerry Kendall. She is the one who is going to be a horticulturist."

Kerry held her breath.

"I say no!" Tracey shouted. "What's with this sudden interest in Kendall anyway, Pam?"

"Oh, I am not interested in her," the other girl protested. "It is just that I have been watching her at lunch time, when she was practicing. She *is* good. She is really good."

Thank you, Pam, Kerry breathed silently.

"Maybe you would like her to replace you?" Tracey sneered.

The other girl was silent. There wasn't a sound from the other side of the partition.

"There are others just as good. And they will look better than she does," Tracey said with finality. "Come on, let's go into the gym."

Before they could exit, Kerry hurried out the door and down the corridor. Andrea was coming out of the office.

"Good grief! I have a stinkeroo of an assignment," she complained. "I have to interview—hey! What's the matter? You look all shook up!"

"Oh, Andrea," Kerry cried. "I haven't a chance! I just heard the varsity squad talking in the girls' room!"

"And?"

"And Tracey Shaffer said I am too tall to make it!"

"Look, Kerry, she is not the only one voting. There are others, too, you know," she said soothingly.

"But don't they usually do as she says? She is the captain, isn't she?"

"Yes, but the others don't always go along with her. Come on, chum. Forget that red-head and let's go into the gym. Let's get it over with."

Nervous and upset, her self-assurance evaporated, Kerry sat rigid on the bleachers until her turn came. Her performance was a fiasco. She forgot some of the words to the Victory Cheer, and, when she leaped into the air after the Fight-Team-Fight cheer, she twisted off-balance and came down in a heap on the floor. Conscious of the sneer on Tracey's face, she limped down to the shower room, Andrea tagging behind her.

"Don't take it so seriously, Kerry," Andrea begged. "So what if you don't make it?"

"Andrea, you *know* that any girl who makes varsity cheer-leading automatically gets invited to join the Crew! And this was my only chance!" she said.

"It might not be. You never know. Let's wait and see before we make a federal case out of this," Andrea said sympathetically. "Come on. Get dressed. Amos will be here in a few minutes."

Ten minutes later, as they waited for Dr. Stark, the varsity cheerleaders came out to the parking lot and got into their cars. None of them even glanced at Kerry.

"You see! I told you!" she stormed. "If I had made it, they would tell me!"

"O.K.! O.K.! So you didn't make it," Andrea agreed.

"But it's important to me!"

"Maybe you wouldn't like that gang anyway."

"But I would! I know I would! You don't know what it means to me, Andrea!"

"You mean—so you can tell Meg or whatever her name is? The one who snagged Tom?" She peered at Kerry in the darkness. "Or is it more than that? I have known kids who wanted to make the Crew, but you—you act as though it is the only thing on earth. Come on, chum. Give. What is it with you?"

"It is more than Meg," Kerry confessed. "All my life I have felt as though I didn't belong somehow. As though my parents were deliberately shutting me off from them. And at the other school I didn't feel that the gang actually considered me one of them. They had all grown up together and I felt as though I—as though they just sort of tolerated me."

"And you think just by being part of THE crowd at Winston High, that you will solve all of your problems. I've got news for you, chum. 'Taint necessarily so. I know."

"What do you mean?"

"Well, I guess I had better tell you before someone else does. I was a member of the illustrious Crew."

"You were?" Kerry clutched Andrea's arm. "You really were? But why didn't you tell me? But why aren't you now? What happened? Did you quit?"

"I didn't quit. Amos made me. He said no one finds herself by retreating into a group, that you have to stand on your own two feet. And he doesn't like what they stand for. He says they are undemocratic, unbearable, uncouth—"

"But why did he let you join in the first place?"

"I told you. He isn't home very often. And it happened when he was away on one of his trips. Sybil doesn't pay too much attention to us as long as she thinks we are fed and clothed," Andrea said bitterly.

There is much I don't know about her, Kerry realized. I have been so concerned with myself and my problems that I haven't given her much of a chance to talk about herself.

At that moment, the lights of a car swept over them as it turned into the parking lot.

"Here is Amos," said Andrea. "Let's go."

When they got into the car, Kerry could just barely discern Dr. Stark in the darkness. Andrea looks like him, she realized. His chubby face was a kindly one; his smile, as they were introduced, was infectious. She found herself smiling back at him.

"Where to, Andrea?" he asked as they pulled slowly out of the school driveway.

"Say!" Andrea said suddenly. "Why don't you come to dinner, Kerry?"

"I couldn't—I—my mother—" she stammered. "Your mother isn't expecting me—"

"Think nothing of it, chum. One or twenty extra. Sybil couldn't care less. She will just tell Maria to pull another steak out of the freezer."

"Maria?"

"The maid. She is quite a gal, isn't she, Amos?"

Dr. Stark nodded.

"She came here from Puerto Rico two years ago to work for us. Sybil and Amos met her when they were down there on vacation. She finished high school, night school, in two years and she is going to college in the fall. She wants to teach."

"She is a very intelligent and ambitious young lady," added Dr. Stark.

"So? Will you come?" Andrea was insistent.

"Maybe I had better go home first and ask Mother."

"Call her from our house and, if she says no, Amos will drive you straight home."

"I guess it will be all right," Kerry agreed reluctantly.

When the car swung into the Stark driveway, Kerry gasped involuntarily, "What a beautiful place!" It was a long redwood house that rambled across the top of a hill. Antique carriage lamps atop poles encircled with ivy illuminated the three terraces of autumn flowers that spread like a gay carpet before the house. A flight of slate steps wound among the gardens to the entrance.

Dr. Stark stopped the car and got out and Andrea slid into the driver's seat. Kerry looked at her in amazement.

"Don't look so surprised!" Andrea laughed.

"Where are we going? I thought you said that your father wouldn't let you drive? That you didn't have a license."

"He won't and I don't, but he lets me drive the car into the garage when we come home." She looked at Kerry. "Don't laugh. It's kid stuff, I guess, but I get a charge out of it. And in a few months, when I am eighteen, I will be driving *out* of the garage, down the hill and away!" she cried as she swung the car around the lawn and up toward the garage.

"I'm not laughing," answered Kerry. "I know how you feel. I get a kick out of driving Old Faithful," she added without thinking.

"Old Faithful?"

Now I've done it, thought Kerry. I might as well tell her. She plunged in. "We don't have a car—just an old truck. That was all Dad was able to salvage from the business."

"You sound as though you were apologizing," Andrea said as they got out of the car. "I think it would be fun to drive a truck. I like anything on wheels. I think I am going to ask for a motor scooter for my eighteenth birthday."

"Oh, no!" laughed Kerry.

"Oh, yes! I mean it. When I am behind the wheel, it makes me feel uninhibited, free as a bird," she said, raising her arms to the side and swooping up the gravel walk that led to the back of the house. "Amos feels the same way when he is skiing he says."

"I know what you mean," Kerry agreed. "Only with me it is swimming. Sometimes when I was out on the lake, I would swim 'way out, turn on my back and float. And the whole world would disappear. There would be nothing. Just me and the sky and the water."

"Amos says everyone needs something like that." She opened the kitchen door and ushered Kerry into an enormous pine-paneled kitchen. It had a floor of red slate; a grey stone planter filled with philodendron separated the work area from the dining area which was surrounded by glass.

"Kerry, this is Maria. Maria, this is Kerry Kendall, my best friend," Andrea said as she put her arm around the slim girl who was standing at the stove.

"How do you do, Kerry," Maria said.

"Hi," Kerry answered, staring at the maid. She was lovely, with white skin and a cloud of soft, shiny black hair.

"What's for dinner?" Andrea asked.

"A casserole," Maria answered. "And soup and salad and a lemon meringue pie. But why the sudden interest in the cuisine?"

They act as though they were sisters, Kerry thought. Maria isn't treated as a servant. That's the way it should be.

"Well, chum," explained Andrea, "Kerry is staying for dinner and I wondered if there would be enough."

"Did you ever know a time when there wasn't enough to eat

in this house? In my country, in Puerto Rico, my whole family could live for a week on what you eat for one dinner."

"Yes, I know, I know. So you're going to finish college and teach and make a lot of money and bring them all up here and they will eat and get fat like me," Andrea chaffed, as she threw her arms about Maria and waltzed her around the kitchen.

"Stop! Stop!" Maria remonstrated. "I have to get the dinner!" She giggled as she extricated herself from Andrea's embrace. "Go! Wash the face and the hands or I won't give you anything to eat!" She pushed the girl toward the door.

Kerry was aware of the deep affection that existed between the two girls. I wish I had a sister, she thought—someone who is like another part of you.

"Come on, Kerry," Andrea ordered. "Maria means it! If we're not ready when she's ready to serve, we will go hungry. She's cruel, cruel, cruel," Andrea teased.

"I will show you how I will be cruel," said Maria. "I will spank you with this," she added, picking up a long loaf of French bread.

"I surrender! I surrender!" Andrea laughed, pulling Kerry with her into the hall.

Andrea's room was almost monastic, with its brown burlap draperies, its studio couch covered with brown burlap, its yellow and brown plaid rug. Funny, Kerry thought, but I would have imagined that her room would be frilly and feminine, more like mine.

"A poor thing, but my own," said Andrea waving her hand

around the room. "I like things around me to be plain and simple. Clothes and make-up—now that's a different thing. I like to look like a female." She paused a moment. "Bathroom is there if you want to wash up," she said abruptly as she kicked off her shoes and flung herself on the bed.

"I wish I had my own bathroom," Kerry called over the sound of running water.

"Why? Isn't there only one of you? You told me that you didn't have any brothers or sisters."

"I know," answered Kerry, drying her hands, "but I just would, that's all."

"It is a necessity for me with four brothers."

"I didn't know that you had four brothers," said Kerry.

"You never asked me, chum," said Andrea, jumping up from the bed.

She hadn't. She had been too busy mulling over her own life, too selfish to care about Andrea, she realized guiltily for the second time that day.

"You will meet them soon enough," Andrea said, stabbing at her hair with a brush. "All four of 'em. And Sybil, my mother," she added coldly.

"Holy cow! I forgot! I have to call my mother," Kerry remembered.

"The 'phone is on the desk. Be my guest."

Mrs. Kendall gave her consent so the two girls went down to dinner.

Kerry stopped and gaped when they entered the living room. It seemed a mile long. Huge rugs, forest green and chartreuse, floated on the polished floor. A large, circular chartreuse couch curved toward a fieldstone fireplace that soared up to the beamed ceiling. Groups of chairs and tables were lost in the void. Floor-length gold draperies shuddered in the breeze from the sliding glass doors on opposite sides of the room.

"It is so—so large," she marveled.

"That is the understatement of the year," laughed Andrea. "Hey, you guys! Ready for dinner?"

Kerry wondered to whom she was speaking. Then she saw them, four small, tow-headed boys, sitting cross-legged in front of a television set at the far end of the room.

All four heads turned simultaneously. "Hi, Andrea," they chorused. And turned back to the screen.

"Come on, small fry. Turn off the switch and get ready for dinner. Come on now and hit the trail, pardners!"

Reluctantly, the boys got up. The smallest one turned off the set and herded the others in front of him.

"Kerry, the men in my family," Andrea said, as they ran toward her. "The big one is Bruce; he is eight. George is six; Tony is five. And this one, this little squirt, is David, going on four," she said, lifting the smallest boy and swinging him around. "Say 'hello' to Kerry, kids."

"Hi, Kerry," they shouted in unison as they scrambled out the door.

CHAPTER IX

Although the atmosphere at dinner was strained for Kerry, she was aware that, for the Stark family, it was not unusual. Mrs. Stark, a placid, plump, faded blonde, greeted Kerry casually and then said not another word to her or to anyone else during the entire meal. Dr. Stark, on the other hand, talked incessantly about everything from politics to television Westerns. Andrea fed him questions and hung on his every answer. The four boys listened, round-eyed, and never uttered a sound. Occasionally he directed words at Mrs. Stark. She smiled, nodded absently and continued eating.

It is so impersonal, Kerry thought; it is almost as though they were all strangers. The coldness was intensified by the decor of the dining room itself. The crystal chandelier glittered icily on the long, shining mahogany table, on the tall, white candles in crystal candelabra, on the dead-white walls. I guess

I never really appreciated how home-like our dining room is, Kerry realized, as she visualized the round cherry table and captain's chairs, the yellow and red calico curtains, the rug, braided in yellow and red and rust. Meals were always pleasant in that cozy room, especially at night when the three of them sat down together and exchanged the day's news over a long, leisurely dinner.

As they got up from the table, Mrs. Stark laid a pudgy hand on Kerry's arm and said softly, "Come again, Mary. Andrea has so few friends." She smiled and drifted off into the living room.

"It is *Kerry,* Sybil, and Andrea has *one* friend," muttered Andrea. "Come on upstairs, chum. You don't have to go right away, do you?"

"No," answered Kerry. "Mom said I could stay 'til eleven, since tomorrow is Saturday."

"Good deal," said Andrea.

They sprawled prone on the floor for an hour, listening to Andrea's jazz records. When Kerry admitted that she knew little if anything about that kind of music, the other girl proceeded to rattle off a complete history of jazz in America. She played some early Ellington, Basie, and Goodman, emphasizing that they were originals; they had belonged to her father when he was in college, and he had handed them down to Andrea.

"Your father doesn't look like a jazz buff," commented Kerry.

"He isn't now. He goes for 'long hair'. He retreats into his study and turns on the hi-fi and he is out of this world. Sybil digs it, too. That is one interest they have in common." She raised herself to a sitting position, rested her chin on her knees and riveted her eyes upon Kerry. "Are you in the mood for a confessional?" she asked speculatively.

Kerry looked up uncertainly. She squirmed mentally. What am I about to hear? I feel uncomfortable. I am not used to eavesdropping on another girl's secret life. Meg and I were good friends but we always held each other at arm's length. We never "exchanged confidences;" I thought that they did that only in Victorian novels. But I want Andrea for my friend; she is the only island in that trackless ocean, Winston High. I would have been lost without her. But will she expect me to reciprocate? Will she expect me to "tell all?" I couldn't!

"Kerry, my friend," Andrea commented dryly, "your face is as a book where men may read strange matters. I could tell everything you were thinking. Shall I listen, you were wondering. Does she expect *me* to let *my* hair down? Will I be able to?"

Kerry grinned. "You and my mother! She can always tell what I am thinking, too!"

"It isn't hard. It is because you are so—so honest. You are naïve. You would have a hard time trying to deceive anyone. Don't ever play poker, chum. And you looked so surprised when I quoted Shakespeare. I read *Macbeth* and a dozen of his plays—on my own. I like to read; I read a lot. I am no moron, Kerry," she insisted.

"I know, Andrea. It wasn't that I was so surprised. It just seemed so out of character."

"You see. You *don't* really know me. That is why I wanted to talk to you, so that you will know me. Maybe you won't like me after all," she concluded quietly.

I am going to listen to her, Kerry decided. She wants desperately to confide in someone. And she won't expect me to open the pages of my diary.

"Fire away. I am all ears," Kerry said.

"I really ought to be horizontal," Andrea giggled. "Amos says that is how some psychiatrists get their patients to relax. He thinks it is silly. He often gets the best results following a patient who is puttering in his garden!"

Was there no end to the unorthodoxy of this family, Kerry wondered.

"I suppose you thought Sybil was rude at dinner tonight?" Andrea began.

"No—I—I—," Kerry hesitated.

"It isn't rudeness, not really. She has just withdrawn from people. She is interested only in babies."

Puzzled, Kerry frowned.

"Don't look so skeptical, chum. It's true. And once the babies are two or three years old, she loses interest. Look, let me fill you in on the long, sad story of the Stark menage." She paused and stared vacantly into space. "You see, Amos met Sybil when he was in England at a psychiatrist's convention. Sybil's father was a vicar and he thought his parishioners could use mental as well as spiritual help so he attended a couple of the meetings. Sybil was with him, Amos saw her, fell like a ton of bricks, and persuaded her to marry him. All in a month! He was quite a handsome guy when he was young. Here, let me show you." She scrambled to her feet, opened her desk drawer and took out a picture. "See? Wasn't he a doll?" she asked, handing the snapshot to Kerry.

A young, good-looking Dr. Stark smiled at the fair, slim girl by his side. "And your mother was lovely," Kerry exclaimed.

"I know," mused Andrea, gazing at the picture. "She had a good figure, her hair was soft and kind of misty blonde, even when I was small." She was silent for a minute, and then, dismissing whatever thoughts had interrupted her story, she continued. "So, anyway, young Lockinvar snatched up his English bride, stowed her away on a plane instead of on a horse, and they came back to the States. I don't think she really knew what hit her. Dragged away from a little English village— Crawling-on-the-Thames—you know those British names—and deposited right smack in the middle of New York City! I guess she was so dazzled by the whole bit she didn't wake up for quite awhile. When I was about nine, in fact."

A knock on the door startled both of them.

"Yes? Who is it?" Andrea asked.

"Us," one of the boys answered.

"That's Bruce," she explained. "He always brings the kids to say good-night. Come on in," she called.

The four boys, pajama-clad, trooped in. Andrea hugged and kissed each one in turn. Dutifully, they said good-night to Kerry and filed out. As they reached the door, David turned, toddled back to Kerry and asked, "I kiss you?" Kerry laughed and hugged him as he planted a damp kiss on her cheek. He stood back, scrutinized her carefully and solemnly announced, "I want you to come back. You are pretty." Then, abashed at his daring, he ran out of the room as fast as his short, fat legs could carry him.

"He is a darling!" Kerry said.

"He is the uninhibited member of this family," Andrea laughed. "But, what was I saying before they came in? Oh, yes, when I was nine, Sybil decided she couldn't take it any longer. She had had enough of the city and she wanted to go back to England—to stay. But Amos couldn't see starting his practice all over again, so they compromised. I guess we traveled a thousand miles before we found this place. You should have seen it, Kerry. It was a regular wilderness, just acres and acres of trees and underbrush and stone walls. But Sybil liked it; she said it looked like England. So Amos bought it and built this house."

"It is perfect," said Kerry. "There must be a wonderful view; you must be able to see for miles and miles."

"You can. That is why Sybil liked it, I guess. She hated being closed in—in New York. That is where she and I are alike. I like space, lots of space. Well, at any rate, we moved. And then Bruce was born. And George and Tony and David. And that is all she has ever done."

"But, Andrea, I don't see what is wrong with having children."

"Nothing, but you don't have them and forget them," she answered bitterly.

"I still don't understand. What do you mean she forgets them?"

"Oh, it is probably Amos' fault, too. As soon as we could walk practically, we went to nursery school, music lessons, dancing lessons, summer camp—the whole bit. Sybil and he argued about it a few years ago, but he insisted we needed—what does he call it—association with our peer group! So Sybil just gave up. He kept insisting she must be a person in her own right, that she mustn't become just a—a hausfrau. But that is what she wants, and he won't let her have it. He wanted her to join clubs and go skiing and all that stuff. Neither of them would give in, so she just sits and reads or gardens. And he goes off skiing or playing tennis. What a happy, happy companionship!" she finished sardonically.

Kerry was silent. I feel sorry for her, she mused. She has money, a beautiful home, lots of clothes; she has all the things that most girls want, that I have never had. And yet, I am better off than she is. No matter what problems I may have, no matter what difficulties I get into, I know that my mother is there to listen to me, to help me, to reassure me.

"Well?" Andrea looked at her questioningly.

"Well—what?" Kerry didn't know what she was expected to say.

"Do you understand me now? And Sybil? And Amos? And the kids? Why they are what they are?"

"Yes, I understand. But you will be away from all this next year. You will be away at college."

"You *don't* understand! It isn't only me! It's all of them I worry about! I *know* I will be away from it all next year, but that is what is bothering me. I feel, and maybe it is just ego, but I feel that I am sort of a balance wheel for the family. You know?"

Kerry nodded.

"I wish I could just stand up to them and say, 'Hey, you two! Why don't you straighten up and fly right?'" She stood up, stretched, and groaned. "Who said adolescence was the happiest time of your life? Whoever he was, he must have been an orphan!"

"Andrea, I am glad you talked it out tonight," Kerry said soberly. "Maybe things will work out. My parents were in a sweat just a month ago; they thought the end of the world had come. Now things are going smoothly. We have never been so happy."

"Ol' Pollyanna Kendall! The darkest hour before the dawn and all that jazz?" Andrea said scornfully.

"You never know," Kerry protested. "Wait and see." She stood up. "And now I had better get going. It is late."

"I hope I haven't bored you," Andrea said sharply.

"Andrea! You know that isn't true! I am flattered that you did tell me. You know that."

"Yes, I do, Kerry. It is just that—well—I have never told all this to anyone before. And I guess I wasn't sure whether you really wanted to hear my confessional."

"I did and I do! You are my friend, my best friend!"

"Thanks, chum." Andrea smiled. "Let's go down and drag Amos away from his Beethoven so he can take you home."

Kerry followed her downstairs and said good-night to Mrs. Stark who was reading. She looked up vacantly, smiled absentmindedly, and returned to her book.

When Dr. Stark dropped Kerry at her house, Kerry raced up the walk. It was good to be home! She stood in the living room door for a moment. This was a doll's house compared to Andrea's mammoth house. But it was home. Her father sat in his old leather chair, his head back and his eyes closed, an open book on his lap. Her mother was curled up on the couch reading.

"Hi! I'm home," she announced.

"So I see," her mother smiled. "Have a good time?"

"Fabulous! You should see! Andrea's house is—is something!"

"Let's save it for tomorrow, shall we? You have to get up early," her mother reminded her. "Remember you said you wanted to plant some bulbs? And you will have to leave after lunch for the football game."

The football game! The cheerleaders! Kerry's face froze. She had forgotten about the tryouts. Strange I haven't thought about them all evening, she wondered.

"What is the matter, Kerry?" her mother asked.

"I didn't make the squad," she muttered.

"I didn't think you did, or you would have told me when you 'phoned. Want to tell me about it?"

"Oh, Mom, I was awful! I goofed! And I shouldn't have! I was good, really good, at practice. Andrea said so."

"What happened?"

"Oh, I heard some of the varsity cheerleaders talking in the girls' room and the captain said she didn't want me. Even before she saw me try out, she didn't want me!"

"The Crew again?" her mother asked.

"Yes, but it was because I am too tall!"

"Oh, Kerry! That's hard to believe! Are you sure?"

"Mother! I *heard* Tracy Shaffer say it!" she exploded.

"All right. All right. Don't get upset. It is over and done with."

"But. I will never make the Crew now! It's the only way—for a girl!" she wailed.

"Kerry," her mother chided, "you must *not* let this ruin your whole senior year. You like Winston; you have already made a place for yourself—the swimming team, homeroom secretary. I think that's pretty good."

"I know all that, but—"

"Look, take your shower and go to bed and get a good night's sleep. You'll feel better in the morning."

Why did mothers always say that? It wasn't true. I will feel worse in the morning, worse in the afternoon when I am a spectator sitting on the bleachers instead of being a cheerleader. I won't be able to stand that! I won't.

"Kerry, didn't you hear your mother tell you to go to bed?" her father's voice startled her.

"Yes, Dad. I am going," she mumbled. "Good night."

She lay awake that night for a long time, re-living her fiasco in the gym. But underneath, in her sub-conscious, was the strange realization that for several hours, while she had been at Andrea's, she had forgotten the whole thing. Was her mother right? Would she feel better in the morning? Maybe.

CHAPTER X

But she didn't feel better next morning. As soon as she awoke, she felt something was wrong. Usually, on Saturday, she reveled in the ten or fifteen minutes she could just lie in bed and think, lazily, what she was going to do that day. But today she was depressed, and, for a few moments, she didn't know why. Until she remembered.

Maybe I will feel better when I get out and work in the garden, she thought, as she pulled on her jeans and shrugged into her sweat shirt. I will spend the whole day working around the place; I won't go to the game. I will think of other things. But she knew it wouldn't work.

After breakfast she dragged the carton of daffodil, tulip and narcissus bulbs from the cellar to the front lawn and started digging. It was a crisp September day, cool, almost chilly in the shade, but pleasantly warm in the sunlight. As she knelt on the ground, an occasional leaf, golden bronze, spiraled down to the lawn. The smell of damp earth was perfume in her nostrils. At least I have this, she reasoned, this talent, if it is a talent, for growing things.

After an hour she sat back on her heels, wiped her sleeve across her perspiring brow, and gazed around. The lawn and the shrubbery looked better now. Her father had planted taxus and azaleas and had trimmed the shaggy lilacs and leggy rhododendron that fringed the house. Mr. Kendall had also seeded the lawn, and it was beginning to show tiny, light-green tips. Like a boy's first beard, Kerry thought.

"Practicing Yoga?" A masculine voice, vaguely familiar, startled her. She tried to get up, but she had been kneeling so long that her legs were numb, and she fell backwards. Two strong arms caught her before she hit the ground.

"Well! I never had a girl fall for me before!" She turned her head awkwardly. It was Mark, Mark Lee. And he didn't seem to want to let her go. He kept his arms around her as she turned to face him. He smiled down at her. Then something happened to his face. A look of surprise, of wonder.

Something is happening to me, too, Kerry thought as she looked up into his wide, dark eyes. I feel—I feel as though I had just had an electric shock. I can't take my eyes away. This must be what it is like when you are hypnotized.

He bent his head slowly, still staring at her. Is he going to kiss me, she wondered. In broad daylight? She was startled. She stiffened and stepped away. Mark's arms dropped to his side.

She turned and stared at him, speechless. Mark stared back. For a long moment.

Then, suddenly, like an anti-climax, they both burst out laughing.

"This isn't exactly the way I planned it," said Mark.

"Planned what?" Kerry asked. She could look at him now, without embarrassment. And somehow, it seemed that she had known him before, that she had always known him.

"I wanted to ask you to join the Runes. Mrs. Grierson—she's our advisor—suggested you at the meeting this week. She said that the theme you handed in this month was good."

"Oh, the description? It was easy; I had a topic that just wrote itself, 'The Aftermath of the Hurricane.'"

"No writing is easy," he said. "I know. I have been at it since I was six."

"Since you were six!"

"I could read when I was four, before I went to school. I am an only child, and I guess I was rather a lonely kid. I wanted to do all the things my parents did. I couldn't stand it when they sat down and read, so I decided I would learn how to decipher all those funny black marks," he laughed.

"Me, too! Except I couldn't stand having *anybody* read when I couldn't. I guess I almost drove my father wild before I went to school. I used to sit on his lap at night and pick out words from his newspaper."

There was an awkward silence after the mutual confessional.

"But I haven't introduced myself!" Mark remembered. "I am Mark Lee, president of—"

"Of the Runes, and you are going to be a writer and you are taking botany because—"

The surprised expression on Mark's face was too much. Kerry couldn't finish; she exploded with laughter and Mark joined her.

"I guess I did sound a little pompous," he admitted. "But I really like Sherry, and I think—I *know*—that he wanted us to give the real reason. I think that he even likes—well, maybe not likes—but I think he respects Stanford for being honest."

"Mm. You're right. And Kenny respects him. That is the only class he does any work in."

"Did you hear what happened in history class with Stanford and Mr. Ford?"

"No. I have Mr. Ford for history, but I wasn't in class the first day. There was some mix-up in my schedule. I did hear that Ford sent Kenny to Mr. Durham."

"And as soon as Bull found out that Stanford was a member of the Crew, he let him off with a reprimand."

"What happened before? In class?"

"The first day Ford asked the class to make out cards, with autobiographical information on them. And when he saw that Ken had gone to a couple of private schools, he announced to the class, 'This young man comes from a private school. We'd better straighten him out.' That was all Ken needed. From then on, it has been open warfare between them. He questions everything Ford says, ties him in knots."

"What a thing to say to a new student! No wonder Kenny battles with him. I noticed that the two of them argue constantly in class."

"Oh, Ford is kookie. We all know that and we act accordingly. He is bright enough; in fact, he is too intelligent to be teaching school. In that school, anyway. He knows his stuff, but he does and says some weird things. Sometimes he does it just to needle the kids, just to shock them into consciousness."

"I noticed that. And I have been afraid that he might single *me* out! But he is a good teacher. I am lucky; I guess I have the best profs in the school—Ford, Grierson, Sherry—"

"That reminds me. Grierson is anxious for you to join the Runes. Will you, Kerry? We really need you."

How can I tell him that I can't, she fretted. I like this boy; I like him a lot. And I want him to like me. I think he does. There is something between us; I could feel it when we looked at each other that first moment. But what will he think of me if I tell him I can't join the Runes because of the Crew?

"Don't look so unhappy," frowned Mark. "I didn't realize that it would make you so miserable."

He's angry, despaired Kerry. What shall I tell him? If I say yes, I will never have a chance to make the Crew. Never. But, if I say no, I may never see him again.

"Could I—would it be possible to let me think it over?" she blurted out.

"Well, all right," he hesitated. "But I don't see what's to think over. It's not such a chore, you know; in fact, it is quite an honor, belonging to our club."

That's not what the Crew thinks, thought Kerry dully.

"Look, if it is a question of time—if you have a lot of other activities, you could just work for the *Winston Week,* the school paper. Then, if you have the time, you could—"

"Oh, it isn't a question of time," she interrupted.

"What is it then?" He waited—then he continued, in a low voice, "Kerry, you will probably think I am—I guess Webster would say—presumptuous. And the kids at school would say—fresh. But it is more than becoming a member of the Runes now. You know that, don't you?"

She looked up at him and thought irrelevantly, he must be over six feet tall. He is one of the few boys I know that I have ever been able to look up at. And to look up to. Because I can.

"Kerry, I am not going to go 'ape' and say that it is love at first sight. But there is something between us. You felt it, too, didn't you? I know you did. I could see it in your face. You did feel it, didn't you?"

She dropped her eyes and murmured, "Yes, Mark."

"I knew it! So, let's forget the Runes for awhile and let me take you to the football game this afternoon. O.K.?"

"I—we—I was supposed to go with Andrea—" she said hesitantly.

"Andrea Stark? Oh, she's a good kid. She'll understand. She won't mind."

"But I promised her."

"Kerry?" her mother called from the doorway. "Are you going to have lunch? Andrea and Dr. Stark will be by to pick you up in an hour." Then she noticed Mark. "I didn't know you had company," she said.

"Come on, Mark. Come and meet my mother," Kerry urged.

"Mother," she said, as Mrs. Kendall opened the screen door for them, "this is Mark Lee. He's president of the Runes. I told you about them. And he has asked me to join the club."

"Wonderful!" exclaimed her mother. "Come in, Mark, and have some lunch."

"No, thank you, Mrs. Kendall. I have to pick my mother up

at the supermarket. But I will take a rain check, if I may," he said, looking at Kerry.

"Of course," Mrs. Kendall smiled.

"I really have to go now," Mark said. "So what time shall I pick you up, Kerry?"

"I can't, Mark," she protested. "I promised Andrea."

"What's the problem?" asked her mother.

"Mark wants to take me to the game, but I can't tell Andrea at the last minute—"

"Why can't the three of you go?" her mother asked.

"Oh, Mother!" Kerry was horrified. Mark will think that she is sending Andrea as a chaperone!

"Sure! Why not?" Mark said eagerly.

"Call Andrea and ask her," Mrs. Kendall suggested.

"Well, O.K., if you think it's all right, Mark," she said reluctantly, as she dialed Andrea's number.

"Why not? I don't often get a chance to squire *two* good-looking girls," he chaffed.

"Andrea?" Kerry asked when the other girl answered.

"Hi, Kerry. What's with you? I was just going to call you. Amos and I will be by to pick you up about 1:15. O.K.?"

"Well, that's what I called about. Mark is here. Mark Lee. And he wants to take—to take us to the game."

"Wants to take *us*? Are you kidding? He wants to take *you*, you mean," Andrea giggled.

"No, Andrea! He really—"

"Forget it, chum. Old Andrea understands." She paused. "How about that? Kerry and Mark. That's a good combination."

"Andrea! Will you listen to me? I want—"

"He's all right, Kerry, really all right. I am glad for you," Andrea said seriously. "But how did it happen? I didn't know that you two knew each other."

"He came over to ask me to join the Runes—and—well, he just asked me to go to the game, that's all," she explained.

"Good deal, chum. Go ahead. I will see you there."

"I won't go unless you do," insisted Kerry.

"Three's a crowd! No, I'll see you at the game. And, Kerry?"

"What?"

"Take him up on the other invitation. Join the club."

"Andrea! I can't. You know it would ruin my chances with the Crew!" she wailed.

"Kerry, forget them. Suppose you hang around all year, waiting for them to give you an invitation into their charmed circle. And suppose they don't come across. You'll be out on a limb. The Runes are O.K., even if they are second-best. And, if you're Mark's steady, there's prestige in that. Maybe not with Raleigh and Shaffer and Kraft. But there are some kids in school who think the academic side is important."

Kerry was silent. Should she? Should she accept Mark's invitation? But what of the Crew? It would be the end for her as far as they were concerned.

"Kerry? Are you still there?"

"Yes," she answered dejectedly.

"Don't sound so glum, chum. Believe me, it's the best thing. If you refuse Mark, you might be left without anything, without any crowd to hang out with. So?"

"Well, I guess so."

"Good deal! Listen, we have parties and picnics. We have fun, really, we do. Oh, not the big brawls that the Crew throws, but we manage."

"Kerry, Mark has to leave," her mother called.

"Be right there, Mother," she answered. "Look, Andrea, I have to hang up. But I wish you would come with us."

"Not a chance. I will see you at the game. And don't feel sorry for me. And quit apologizing. I can snag my own man," she boasted. "So long."

"Andrea won't come with us," she said as she returned to the living room.

"Maybe she will let me buy her a Coke," Mark laughed, "even though she doesn't want to be seen with me in public."

"Oh, Mark, it isn't that!" Kerry protested.

"I know," answered Mark. "I was only joking. I know Andrea. She is one of the most reliable reporters on the staff. And a very determined character. Ask Duke about her."

"Duke! Duke Kraft?"

"The same. They went steady for a while."

"Duke and Andrea?" Kerry could not believe her ears.

"Ask her about it, some time," suggested Mark. "And now I had better be going. Mom will wonder where I am. I told her I would be back in half an hour."

"Good-bye, Mark. Come again," Mrs. Kendall said.

"Thank you, Mrs. Kendall. And I will be back at 1:15 for you, Kerry. O.K.?"

"I guess so," she faltered. "And, Mark, I have made up my mind. I will join the Runes."

He smiled. "I thought you would," he said as he left.

After he had gone, she flung herself on the couch, next to her mother.

"Mom, I don't know whether I did right or not," she admitted.

"You mean about Andrea? Frankly, I did think that you should have gone with her. After all, you did make plans."

"No, it isn't that. It's the Runes. Mark asked me to become a member, to write for the school paper—and maybe for the magazine and the *Tatler,* the year book."

"Why, that's wonderful! I'm glad! But why do you think you made a mistake? I don't understand." Her mother was puzzled.

And then Kerry told her the whole story, about the Crew, about their ostracism of anyone that didn't belong to their clique.

"Kerry," her mother began thoughtfully, "I think you made a wise move. You wouldn't really belong to that clique."

"You mean—because we don't have money and—"

"No, that isn't it at all. I mean you—Kerry—you might be accepted by them, but I don't believe you would accept them. I think they are running scared; I think they are insecure. Most adolescents are. And they huddle together in clubs and gangs. You know—us against the world. It's perfectly normal, but it becomes a dangerous thing when it results in something like the Crew. From what you say, they are not only on the defensive; they are on the offensive. They can't be content just with being exclusive; they have to be aggressive about their uniqueness. That can lead to trouble. And I don't think you would want any part of that."

"I don't know what you mean, Mother," Kerry said.

"We will talk about it some other time," her mother promised. "Now," she said, getting up, "hadn't you better have some lunch and get ready? Mark will be back before you know it." She stood looking down at Kerry. "You know, Kerry, I like Mark."

Kerry smiled. "I do, too."

CHAPTER XI

Mark and Kerry arrived at the school just as the band was marching on to the field. Attired in brand-new navy and white uniforms, the musicians stepped smartly down the gridiron. When they reached the fifty-yard line, they swung toward the Winston bleachers and played the Alma Mater. As the last strains of the song faded down the field, the varsity team, clad in navy satin uniforms, trotted out on the field. The band swung into a syncopated "Hail the Conquering Hero Comes," but the roar from the cheering stands drowned out the music.

As the teams lined up for the kick-off, Kerry and Mark hurried across to the bleachers. There didn't seem to be an inch of empty space; it appeared that not only the whole student body but also the entire town had turned out for the first game.

"Let's sit on the top shelf," suggested Mark, guiding Kerry as they threaded their way up the wooden tiers.

Kerry would have preferred to sit on the bottom row. I feel so conspicuous, she fretted. It would have been better if he and I had our first date at a dance or had gone to a movie. Then everyone would have gotten used to us as a couple. Then a small, inner voice asked, "Who says you are going to *be* a 'couple'? He hasn't asked you to go steady." But I know he will, she told herself smugly. I *know!*

As they squeezed into seats at the top of the grandstand, Andrea came struggling up after them. "Boy! What a crowd!" she spluttered as she wedged herself alongside of Kerry.

"So you did come after all?" Kerry said happily.

"I said I would, didn't I? Old Reliable, that's me." She leaned across Kerry. "Hi, Mark."

"Hi, Nelly Bly," he answered.

"Who is Nelly Bly?" Kerry asked.

"A girl-type reporter who went 'round the world back in the good old days when women were supposed to be the weaker sex," explained Andrea.

"*Supposed* to be?" teased Mark.

"Now, let's not get into a discussion of the natural superiority of women," Andrea answered. "Let's watch the game."

Kerry felt a twinge of resentment at the camaraderie between the two. Am I jealous? Of Andrea? Or is it simply that I don't feel secure yet? I am not sure of Mark. This is only a football date. Maybe it will be our only one. She moved closer to Mark. He looked down at her, smiled, linked arms with her, and continued to watch the players on the field.

Strange, thought Kerry, as she watched the cheerleaders prancing up and down, their white skirts swinging in rhythm, strange that the hurt, the disappointment at not making the squad, is beginning to fade. Why? I wanted to die when I failed. But now it seems like something that happened long ago. It must be Mark. Meeting him has made me forget.

Bracketed by Andrea and Mark who whooped at every foot of turf that Winston gained and groaned at every inch lost, Kerry found herself caught up in the excitement. Never one to get involved at school games, she discovered that a victory for the team meant a great deal to her. Somehow she felt a part of Winston High. She leapt to her feet and yelled at the top of her hungs when Duke Kraft, the quarterback, made a touchdown. As a result of her hours of practice, she knew every cadence, every nuance of the cheers. Unconsciously, she performed every gyration, and the spectators around her caught her spirit. Soon they were watching and following her instead of the cheerleaders on the field.

When the half had ended and Mark had left to buy refreshments, Andrea turned slowly to Kerry and asked, "What are you? A one-woman cheerleading squad?"

Breathless, Kerry answered, "I guess I know what school spirit is now!"

"You sure do, chum! But you had better take it slow and easy. There are a few characters who don't appreciate your school spirit," she said mysteriously.

"What are you talking about? Who?"

"Tracey Shaffer, for one."

"Tracey Shaffer? Why should she—"

"You were taking the limelight away from her, chum. This whole section of the stand was watching you and listening to you."

"Oh, really, Andrea!"

"She has been looking daggers at you, the whole second quarter. She will think of some way to get back at you. You'll see. I did."

"What did she do to you?"

"It's a long story." She was silent, watching the band perform some intricate maneuvers on the gridiron.

"Andrea! Tell me. I hate people who tease by telling part of—"

"O.K. But it isn't that important. It was Duke—and I. We went steady two years ago."

"You and Duke? Duke Kraft?"

"Yes, I and Duke Kraft. Don't look so surprised. Did you think I never had a boy friend? I may not be any Miss America, but I'm not exactly ugly, either—"

"Oh, Andrea! You know I think you're attractive! It isn't that. It's just that—Duke Kraft! He doesn't seem to be your type."

"Why not?"

"You told me yourself. He's wild, conceited."

"He isn't really, 'way down deep, I mean. He's just getting back at the world, at his family, really."

"What for?"

"Amos would say it was sibling rivalry. He's jealous of his two older brothers, 'tho he won't admit it. They were both Phi

Beta at college and they are both successful lawyers. Duke doesn't even want to go to college."

"But why?"

"He wants to join the Air Corps, right after graduation."

"I'd think he'd be better off going to college and then going into the service."

"No, not Duke. College would be a waste of time for him. He's like me. He doesn't like restrictions; he wants freedom, space to breathe. Sometimes, when we were going steady, he used to frighten me. And I don't frighten easily. He souped up his car and, once, out on the new parkway cut-off he had it up to 120 miles an hour."

"You were with him?"

"Yes. He said it was the closest he had ever been to flying."

"Andrea! You might have been killed!"

"So? I'm a fatalist, chum. You know, like the Greeks—those three characters that sit up there and weave the threads of my life. And some day—snip! I'm dead."

Kerry was puzzled. I never realized she thought this way. She's sarcastic; she jeers at things. But lots of kids are that way, especially when they get to be seniors. It's the thing to do.

"Well, anyway," Andrea continued, "the Duke and I were kindred spirits. It wasn't just physical. We liked the same books, the same people. We even liked the same food. We both hated liver, spinach, fried eggs, and rice pudding," she ticked off on her fingers.

"Then I don't see why—"

"The Crew, chum, the Crew. When Amos insisted I withdraw from the holy circle, Duke gave me the brush. Just like that," she said, flicking her fingers on her sleeve.

"You mean, he thought more of them than he did of you?"

"It wasn't that, Kerry. All his friends were in. A boy can't be a loner."

"Mark is."

"Mark is different. He has a lot on the ball. He can write; he has talent. He doesn't need anyone. He has never needed anyone—up until now."

"Up until now?"

"Don't be modest, chum. He really likes you."

"Oh, Andrea. This is our first date—and it may be our last."

"Don't you believe it. He's been talking to me about you ever since that first day he saw you in botany class. You're the only girl he ever showed any interest in—except for one other, when he was a freshman."

"Who, Andrea?"

"Tracey. Tracey Shaffer."

"Oh, no!" I hate her, thought Kerry. I hate any girl that Mark ever liked.

"Oh, yes. But she brushed him off when he turned down an invitation to join the charmed circle. She did her best to force him to accept, but, you know Mark. Or, at least, you will. He wouldn't have anything to do with them." She paused for a moment. "Unfortunately, Duke didn't have the intestinal fortitude to drop out," she added disconsolately.

"And Duke and Tracey? They started going steady?"

"Mm. Just as soon as she found out that he and I had called it quits. He still used to come over to the house once in a while.

I didn't mind. But when she found out, she threatened to have him excommunicated."

"Just for coming to see you?"

"Sure. I told you—the Crew—it's just like sororities and fraternities in college. If you belong to a certain fraternity, you date only the sorority girls they think are acceptable."

"It's not fair!"

"What is? Just be glad Mark had the courage to refuse—"

"Do I hear my name being taken in vain?" Mark laughed as he stepped gingerly between the spectators in front of them. "Here you are, ladies, something for the inner man—or woman, I should say," he said, as he handed them Cokes and frankfurters.

Andrea wolfed down her food, explaining, "I'm starved!"

Kerry ate slowly, thinking over what Andrea had just told her. Maybe I was lucky, she decided. If I had made the cheering squad and had been invited to join the Crew, I wouldn't have been able to date Mark. Would I have been able to turn them down for him? She stole a glance at him. I would! I would! But, down deep, she wasn't quite sure.

Still thinking about Andrea's revelation, she was subdued during the third quarter. But when the last quarter started, she came to life again. The other team made a touchdown and tied the score. The spectators rose to their feet and roared.

A few minutes later Duke intercepted a pass and, swiveling around left end, streaked down the field to a touchdown. The crowd surged down off the bleachers toward the Winston goal. Duke kicked the point after touchdown and, as the ball spiraled between the goalposts, the whistle blew, ending the game.

Linking arms, Mark, Andrea and Kerry snake-danced around the field with the rest of the students. The band retreated to the empty bleachers and struck up the Alma Mater. Eventually the entire school massed before them, shouting the song at the top of their lungs.

"Let's get out of this bedlam," Andrea screamed in Kerry's ear. "If we don't leave now, we will never get a seat in the Hut."

"What is the Hut?" yelled Kerry.

"The local malt shop. Everybody goes there after games."

Using Mark as a battering ram, they managed to thrust themselves through the milling throng. When they arrived at the Hut, there were few empty seats.

"There isn't much room now," noted Kerry. "What happens when the mob gets here?"

"You'll see," Andrea said abruptly.

"Let's order and get out of here before they do get here," suggested Mark.

Kerry was puzzled. It was fun to celebrate a victory with the rest of the students; she was looking forward to it. But Mark and Andrea were anxious to leave. Why?

Ten minutes later, as she was sucking the last bit of syrup from the bottom of her glass, the door banged open and the cheerleading squad, led by Tracey, swept in. The captain swaggered over to the first table which was occupied by freshmen. Hands on hips, she ordered scornfully, "Up, creeps!"

The students were dumb-founded. None of them spoke or moved.

"Did you hear me, chippies? Up! And out!" she said, jerking her manicured thumb over her shoulder. "The Hut is ours!"

"What does she think she is doing?" whispered Kerry.

"Whenever the Crew comes in, they make other kids vacate if there isn't enough room. And sometimes when there is," said Mark bitterly.

"And the other kids stand for it?"

"Watch," said Andrea.

Slowly and silently, the freshmen slid out of their seats and filed out the door. Without waiting for Tracey's orders, most of the students at the other tables vacated their seats also. In a few minutes, all of the tables were occupied by the Crew.

"Let's go," suggested Mark.

"No!" Kerry said suddenly. "Why should we let them put us out?"

"They are not putting us out, Kerry. I just want to leave. Come on," he urged, pushing his chair back.

"Well, they will think they are putting us out," grumbled Kerry. "It is pretty obvious, isn't it? For us to leave when they come in?"

"Forget it, chum. Who cares what they think?" Andrea answered.

As they passed Tracey's table, she looked up, wide-eyed, at Mark and purred, "Hi, Mark." She ignored the girls completely.

"Hi," he muttered, without looking at her.

"It was some game, wasn't it, Mark?" she persisted, reaching up and trailing her fingers down his sleeve as he passed.

Mark jerked his arm away and didn't answer. When they reached the sidewalk, he turned to Kerry and apologized. "I— she doesn't—"

"It's O.K., Mark," Andrea laughed. "I told Kerry that you went steady with her when you were a freshman and didn't know better."

"Thanks, friend," Mark said. "Then there is no explanation necessary?" He squeezed Kerry's hand.

"None, Mark," Kerry smiled up at him.

"Good girl," he said softly and left to get the car.

"Thanks for telling me, Andrea. I might have been jealous if I hadn't known. In fact, I think I am a little jealous anyway—that he did like her once. She's pretty attractive, with that flaming red hair and those sea-green eyes."

"That she is," admitted Andrea. "But how do you think I feel? Mark is safe from her; he doesn't even like her. But Duke . . ."

"I'm sorry, Andrea. I wasn't thinking—except about myself," Kerry apologized.

"Hey, you two!" Mark called as he pulled up to the curb.

As they piled into the front seat, Kerry suggested, "Why don't you take me home first, Mark? Otherwise you'll have to go to Andrea's and all the way over to the other side of the town."

"Don't be naïve, chum," interrupted Andrea. "Our hero hasn't had a chance to say a word to you today. Me and my big mouth. Don't you think he wants to get you alone?"

"Oh, Andrea!" Kerry blushed.

"Maybe you had better come along," Mark teased. "To protect her from my villainy."

"Stop it, you two!" Kerry said.

But I like it, she admitted, as she snuggled down in the seat between Mark and Andrea. What more could a girl want? A best girl friend and a best—a steady, maybe—boy friend.

It was almost dark when they reached Andrea's house. As they swung out of her driveway, Kerry moved away from Mark.

"Hey! What's the matter?" he asked. "Where are you going?"

"I just thought—there is more room now that Andrea—" she stammered.

"I don't drive with my arms spread out," he chuckled. "And don't worry about my driving with one hand. I wouldn't even if it were my own car."

"Whose is it?" Kerry asked, sliding back to the middle of the seat.

"My mother's. Which reminds me, Kerry. I wanted to take you to the movies tonight, but Mother has to use the car. And I won't be able to come over to your house."

"I guess not, Mark! It is a three-mile walk!" She was disappointed but she knew it was impossible.

"This will probably be the only Saturday that Mother will have to use the car. I will have it every week-end from now on. So?"

"So?" Is he asking me to go steady? She held her breath.

"So will I see you every Saturday?"

"If you want to," she answered softly.

"You know I do."

Neither of them said another word until Mark pulled up at the gate. Then Mark put his hands on her shoulders, turned her toward him, and said, "May I kiss you, Kerry?"

Wordlessly, she lifted her face to his. He bent down and kissed her. A firm, brief kiss. She was speechless. Her lips tingled; her whole body tingled. It was like the first dazzle of sunrise, like the first shimmer of starlight.

Suddenly Mark leaned back, frowning.

"What is the matter, Mark?" Was he disappointed that she had permitted him to kiss her on their first date? There were boys like that, boys who would kiss and tell. Did Mark think she was cheap? Did he think she permitted every boy this liberty? I should tell him that Tom is the only other date I have ever kissed. But what would he think? Would he believe me? I don't want to lose him!

"There is nothing the matter," he answered slowly. "It is just that I think that you had better go into the house or your mother will wonder where you are."

He does think it! Why didn't I refuse, she thought as she slid quickly across the seat and out of the car.

"Kerry!" he called as she ran up the drive. "Kerry, I will 'phone you tonight."

But she didn't answer. She couldn't. He would have heard the tears in her voice.

CHAPTER XII

She stood on the porch for a long minute, re-arranging her thoughts and her face. I can't let Mom and Dad see me like this, she realized. She forced a smile and opened the door.

They were eating dinner when she walked into the house.

"I am sorry that I am late," she apologized. "But we stopped at the Hut for a soda and then we had to take Andrea home."

Neither of them answered her. What is the matter now, she wondered, as she ran upstairs to freshen up. Are they angry because I am a little late? If they only knew how upset *I* am! This isn't like them. They look annoyed. Or is it worry?

"Mm! Baked beans and Boston brown bread! And straw-berries and cream for dessert! Good! I am starved!" she ex-claimed as she sat down at the table.

"Kit," Mr. Kendall began, laying down his fork, "aren't you going to tell her?"

"Not now, Brad. After dinner," her mother answered.

"Tell me what? What, Mom?" Kerry asked anxiously.

"Later, Kerry. Finish your meal," her mother ordered.

Here we go again, Kerry thought. They are walling themselves in, erecting a barrier again. And I thought that was all over. They promised.

"There! I am finished!" she announced presently, as she spooned up the last strawberry. "Can I hear now?"

"Kerry, Grandma is coming to live with us," her mother said.

"Oh, no! She is not coming *here!*" Kerry wailed. Then realizing how she sounded, she clapped her hand over her mouth and looked, horror-stricken, at her father.

"What do you mean 'oh, no!'? Who do you think you are? To decide whether your grandmother is going to live here?" her father stormed.

"Brad! Brad! She doesn't know! I haven't told her."

"She ought to have her mouth slapped, big as she is," he thundered.

"I'm sorry, Dad. I—I didn't mean it," Kerry stammered.

"You talk to her, Kit. I'm going to have my coffee in the living-room!" Hands shaking, he picked up his cup and saucer and strode out.

"Mom, I didn't know what I was saying. Really, I didn't. And you know why I reacted the way I did, without thinking. Ever since you told me what a rough time you had, when you lived with Grandma . . ."

"I know. And I should have prepared you for it."

"But why, all of a sudden, did she decide to come here? Why?"

"She had a slight heart attack this afternoon, and the doctor says she shouldn't be alone in that big house."

"Heart attack! A real one? Or faked, like her headaches?"

"Kerry!"

"Well, you know her. Maybe she just did this so she could come here. Maybe she got tired of—"

"Kerry! I don't want you to talk that way! She would never leave the old home unless she was forced to. I told you. That is why Dad and I had to go live with her after we were married. She just refused to give up her house."

Everything was spoiled now, Kerry brooded. There would be no more happiness, no more fun for the three of them.

"Things aren't going to change," her mother promised. "Go in and tell Dad you are sorry."

"Oh, Mom! I'd rather wait 'til you come in with me!"

"All right, but let's get the dishes done in a hurry. There is so much to be done."

When the kitchen chores were completed, Kerry asked anxiously, "What will I say to him? I've never seen him so angry before, Mom."

"He's worried, Kerry. Even tho' the doctor said Grandma's condition isn't serious, that she will live for years if she takes care of herself, Dad is worried. And I think he knows that— that it won't be too easy for me, having to adjust all over again. That bothers him, too."

"That's what bothers me, Mom. She will want to take over, the way she did before."

"I don't think so. This is my house," her mother smiled. "And she will be a guest. Let's go in and tell Dad that she will be a welcome guest," she said, taking Kerry by the arm.

Mr. Kendall was sitting in his chair, his coffee untasted on the table beside him, the newspaper still folded and unread on his lap. He was staring vacantly into space.

"Brad?" her mother said softly, sitting on the couch opposite him. She motioned Kerry to sit beside her.

"Yes?" he answered dully, not looking at them.

"Brad, Kerry wants to say something to you."

"What does she want to say?" he asked in a monotone.

He looks so tired and sad, so defeated, Kerry realized. I am ashamed of how I acted at dinner. If I could only take back the words I said! But you never can. I will think before I speak from now on, she vowed.

"Dad," she pleaded, "please forgive me. I don't know why I said what I did. I didn't know Grandma was sick. I am sorry. And I am glad that she is coming—so that we can take care of her. I will help all I can."

Her father turned his head slowly. He seemed to have difficulty in focusing his eyes upon her.

"Dad? Did you hear me?"

"I heard you," he answered lifelessly.

"Oh, Dad!" she cried, kneeling beside him, resting her head on his chest. Tears trickled down her cheeks onto his shirt.

He sighed, a deep sigh from the bottom of his heart, and

put his arms around her. "Everything will be all right, Kerry. Stop crying."

"Here, here!" her mother joked. "Look what you're doing to Dad's clean shirt!"

Kerry looked up at him. He smiled down at her, took a handkerchief from his pocket and dried her tears. It *is* going to be all right, she thought, getting up to sit beside her mother. Mom always makes things come out all right.

"Now!" Mrs. Kendall began briskly. "We have a lot to talk about and a lot to do. Where shall we begin, Brad?"

"Well, I will have to see a real estate man tomorrow about the house. Those big places are a drug on the market, so we might have trouble finding a buyer."

"Grandma's going to sell her house?" Kerry asked incredulously.

"She has to. I told you that she can't—that the doctor said she mustn't work so hard," her mother reminded her.

"But she won't like that, will she? Didn't you say that she vowed she would never leave there?" Kerry probed.

"She has no choice," Mr. Kendall explained. "Of course, she isn't going to like it. She isn't going to like the idea of living with us any more than you do, Kerry," he finished bitterly.

"Brad, she said she was sorry," her mother reminded him gently.

"But there are some things in life over which we have no control. Things we have to do, like it or not," he said. "We are all just going to have to adjust, Grandma as well as the three of us."

"What about the furniture, Brad?" her mother asked.

"It will have to be sold, of course. But that isn't any problem. Any antique dealer would be glad to get his hands on it."

"We certainly haven't any room for any of it here," her mother said. "It's so big."

"She won't like parting with her bed. It's over a hundred years old. Remember her telling us how Grandma Kendall and my father were born in that bed and that she refused to go to the hospital when I was born?"

"You were born there?" Kerry asked.

"I was. In fact, we had a hard time persuading her that you shouldn't be!" He laughed.

"Dad, why couldn't Grandma have my other bed? I don't need two," Kerry said.

"That's a good idea," Mrs. Kendall agreed. "And then Grandma could bring her dresser and a few small pieces, her spinet desk and chair. Our spare room is large enough for those."

"Then it would seem more like home to her," Kerry added.

"I will tell her what you said, Kerry," her father promised. "She will like that." He got up and started for the hall. "Coming, Kit?"

"Where are you going?" Kerry asked.

"To Grandma's," her mother answered.

"Isn't she in the hospital?"

"No, the doctor said it would be better if she stayed at home, until she comes here. There's a nurse with her, day and night," her mother explained. "But Dad and I are going over to see her now. Do you want to come?"

"I—I—do I have to?" Kerry stammered. "I'm expecting a 'phone call—"

Her father turned abruptly. "A 'phone call! That's more important than going to see your grandmother?" he thundered.

"Kerry, I don't think any telephone call is so urgent that it can't wait," her mother chided.

But it is, Kerry thought. It is! It's from Mark! How can I tell them?

"Is it from Mark?" her mother whispered.

Kerry nodded.

"We won't be long," Mrs. Kendall promised. "We will be back before nine o'clock. When he calls and there is no answer, he will call back."

"O.K.," Kerry agreed reluctantly.

When they arrived at her grandmother's house, it was dark except for a light in an upstairs window. Mr. Kendall unlocked the door, reached for the switch on the wall and snapped on the hall light. You would never know Grandma was sick, Kerry observed as she followed her parents upstairs. Everything is waxed and polished as usual.

Her grandmother was sitting up in the enormous mahogany bed, propped up on pillows. Newspapers were spread before her, a book lay open at her elbow, and a half-finished sweater and knitting needles were directly in front of her. A gray-haired nurse sat beside the bed, reading a magazine.

"It's good to see you, Brad," she smiled as she turned her cheek for Mr. Kendall's kiss. "Hello, Kit—Kerry." She merely nodded at them and held out her hand to her son. "Here, sit here, on the bed, Brad," she directed.

"Mother! What's all this?" he asked, nodding at the papers, the book and the knitting. "I thought the doctor told you to rest!"

"Rest! He's an old fool! Can't change the habits of a life-time, just because I had a little fainting spell!"

"Fainting spell? Mother!" Mr. Kendall shook his head. "You know—"

"All right, Brad. I'll behave." She glanced up at Kerry and her mother. "Don't stand there, you two. Sit down."

Kerry and her mother sat on the two horsehair chairs at the foot of the bed.

"Oh, Miss—Miss—what-ever-your-name-is," she said to the nurse. "Why don't you go for a walk or something? Until my son leaves. Come back about eleven o'clock," she ordered.

The nurse looked questioningly at Mr. Kendall.

Eleven o'clock! Kerry's heart sank. Mark would never call that late!

"Don't worry," her mother whispered. "We won't be staying that late."

"What are you two whispering about?" the elder Mrs. Kendall asked, peering at them sharply.

"I was just saying, Mother Kendall, that you do need your rest," Kerry's mother answered calmly. "Miss Wareham," she continued, looking at the nurse, "we will be here until eight-thirty. Why don't you take a break and come back then?"

The nurse nodded and left the room.

"Brad! I want you to stay until eleven," the elder Mrs. Kendall pouted. "It gets lonely when there's nothing to do."

"Now, Mother," he reminded her. "You never stay up that late. The nurse will give you a sleeping pill and you'll go right off."

She agreed reluctantly and then proceeded to talk with her son, ignoring Kerry and her mother completely. At eight-thirty, Miss Wareham returned and bustled around the room, getting ready to prepare her patient for the night. In a few minutes, Kerry and her mother were on their way downstairs while Mr. Kendall was listening to some last-minute instructions from his mother.

"Mom, it isn't going to be easy, is it?" Kerry said.

"No, it isn't," her mother agreed. "But it will work out, Kerry. You'll see," she promised, putting her arms around her daughter.

On the way home, no one said a word until they reached the drive. Then Mr. Kendall explained, "I will leave the truck here, instead of parking it in the garage. Just in case."

The telephone rang as Kerry opened the door. Without removing her coat, she ran down the hall and picked up the receiver.

"Hello?"

"Kerry?" It was Mark. "Where have you been? I have been trying to get you for an hour!"

"Oh, Mark!"

"Hey! What is wrong? You sound strange."

"We just got back from my grandmother's. She is ill. She had a heart attack today."

"A heart attack! I am sorry. I won't keep you."

"No! Don't hang up, Mark! I feel better talking to you. It wasn't a serious attack. She will be all right if she just slows down. But she has to come to live with us!"

"You sound as though you don't like the idea," Mark said curtly.

"You don't understand! It is such a mess!" How could she explain to him? He would think her cruel and unfeeling.

"Listen, Kerry, let me call you tomorrow. You are upset now. If there is anything I can do, let me know, will you?"

"All right. I guess you are right. I am not very coherent to-night." Partly because I don't know what happened to us this afternoon, she thought. "Better call around noon. That is when we have dinner on Sunday. The rest of the day, I don't know . . ."

"I understand. And Kerry?"

"Yes, Mark?"

"I have something to tell you when I see you. Good-night," he said softly.

"Good-night, Mark."

She replaced the telephone, took off her coat, and slowly climbed the stairs. I have never had a day like this in my life, she decided. Happiness and sorrow. Mark and Grandma. If this is adulthood, I am afraid.

CHAPTER XIII

After breakfast the next morning, Mr. and Mrs. Kendall went to the elder Mrs. Kendall's house to inventory the furniture. As Kerry was starting to prepare dinner the telephone rang. It was too early for Mark to call; it was only eleven o'clock.

It was Andrea. When Kerry related the events of the previous evening, she expressed her sympathy.

"Is there anything I can do to help, Kerry?" the other girl inquired.

"No, thanks. Not now, anyway."

"Listen, maybe I could come over and get meals?"

"That is what I am doing now. Mom and Dad went over to Grandma's to make a list of the furniture."

"Hey, chum? Didn't you tell me once that your grandmother had some Victorian things?" She sounded excited.

"Yes. Why?"

"Sybil flips over that stuff. Her bedroom looks like Queen Victoria's! She was always going to furnish the living room—the whole house, in fact, in mahogany and velvet and fringe. But, with four boys, you know how long that would last."

"But she wouldn't want it now, would she?"

"She could store it. The garage is overflowing with antiques she has picked up in her meanderings. Do you think your father would mind if Sybil went over to look at it? Just to look?"

"I—I don't know. Maybe I had better ask him first."

"Do that, and call me back?"

"Well, he won't be home until noon, and Mark is going to call . . ."

"So call me after Mark calls you. What happened last night?"

"Last night?"

"When he brought you home, chum!"

"Nothing. Nothing happened. What could have happened?"

"Don't play dumb. You mean he didn't even kiss you good-night? Didn't even try?"

"No," Kerry lied. She could not tell her things like that, she thought. Not personal things about Mark. Somehow she knew that he wouldn't like it.

"How about that! The old boy must be losing his grip."

"Andrea!"

"I'm kidding, Kerry," she said seriously. "Mark is all right. More than all right. But don't expect him to be like other boys. He's different. He's—I guess you would call it—more mature than the other kids. Everything has to be done according to protocol; everything has to be thought about, speculated on, planned to the last detail. I'll bet he is figuring out now when he's going to kiss you for the first time."

If she only knew! Kerry thought smugly.

"Kerry?"

"What?"

"You don't mind my—this character analysis of Mark, do you? I like him and I like you. And I'm glad that you two got together."

"I know you are, Andrea. And I don't mind. Why should I? The more I know about him, the better. I don't think he is the kind to talk too much about himself."

"Right! Half the time you don't know what he is thinking."

"I am used to that. My dad is like that. But, I know what I am thinking! If I don't finish getting dinner—"

"O.K. I will wait for your call this afternoon. So long."

When Mr. and Mrs. Kendall came home to dinner, Kerry told them about Mrs. Stark's interest in her grandmother's furniture and her father suggested that Andrea's mother meet them at the old house.

Kerry didn't want to leave the house before Mark called, so she dwadled with the dishes, drying each one carefully. Finally her father threatened to make her walk to her grandmother's unless she hurried. Just as she finished stacking the dishes in the closet, Mark called.

"I can't talk, Mark. I have to go over to Grandmother's," she explained.

"I understand," he said. "I had hoped to see you today, but I guess it's impossible. There is something I wanted to tell you."

"I know. You mentioned it last night."

"Who is that?" her father demanded impatiently. "Who's on the 'phone?" He stood at the door, ready to go.

"It's Mark," answered Kerry.

"Mark? Mark who?"

"Oh, Dad! The boy I went to the football game with yesterday. He just called to see if there is anything he can do to help." She couldn't think of anything else to say. And, besides, she convinced herself, Mark did offer yesterday.

"How big is he?" her father asked thoughtfully.

"How big is he?" What was the matter with her father? Why was he asking that?

"Yes. Is he big and strong?"

"I—I—guess so." She was thoroughly confused. Grandma's illness must have affected him.

"Well, he *can* help. If Mrs. Stark decides to buy the furniture, I can deliver it to her, but I'll need someone to help me. Do you think this—this Mark would—"

"He will, Dad!" she interrupted eagerly. "Mark? Mark?"

"Hey! I hear you! Don't shout!" he laughed.

"Mark, Dad wants to know—"

"I heard him, Kerry," Mark broke in. "Tell him I'm all brawn and no brain and I'd be glad to help him."

"Dad—Dad! He says he—Mark says he—"

"I take it he is agreeable," her father concluded. "Well, come on then. Tell him we will meet him there."

"Mark, can you—do you have the car today? Dad wants you to meet us there."

"I have the car, but where's 'there'?"

"Oh, I am stupid!" she babbled. "Of course you don't know. How could you? How would you know where my grandmother—"

"Hey! Take it easy! Simmer down. Just tell me where I am supposed to go," he said.

What is the matter with me, she wondered. I'm so excited I can barely talk, just at the prospect of seeing Mark. He will think I am an idiot! And what does Dad think? He was staring at her rather sternly. I had better calm down.

Taking a deep breath, she said, calmly, "Do you know where Oak Street is, Mark?"

"Sure. A couple of blocks from the school."

"Well, the house is about half way down, on the right, coming from Main. It's a great big house, with a greenhouse on the side."

"Just tell him the truck will be parked outside," her father suggested. "And come on, Kerry! It's getting late!"

"I heard him," said Mark. "The truck will be parked outside. I'll find it. See you in a few minutes."

When they reached the old house, Mark was already there. He shook hands with Mr. Kendall and followed them into the house.

"What a beautiful old place!" he exclaimed as he walked into the living room.

Mr. Kendall was pleased. "I thought the younger generation went for angles and cubes," he commented.

"I don't sir," answered Mark, slowly rubbing his hands over the intricately carved chairs. "There is warmth and security in this, and in this house. It has roots."

"I know what you mean, Mark. I feel the same way," Mr. Kendall agreed quietly.

Kerry stared at the boy. No wonder Andrea said he was different! If another boy had made the statement Mark had, I would think he was pretentious, pompous, trying to impress Dad. But Mark is frank, unaffected. Dad knows that, too. Dad likes him!

After Mr. and Mrs. Kendall had gone upstairs, Kerry took Mark on a tour of the house. He gazed in awe at the high-ceilinged rooms, the cavernous marble fireplaces, the lofty windows. In the library he stood speechless before the tall, spacious shelves crammed with books.

When her father called to her to come up to see her grandmother, she insisted that Mark come also. Reluctantly he followed her upstairs and waited in the hall.

"Dad," she called, "could you come out here for a minute?"

When he appeared in the doorway, she whispered, "Is it all right if Mark comes in to see Grandma?"

Her father frowned.

"Who is that out there?" her grandmother shrilled.

"It is I, Kerry, and Mark," Kerry answered boldly.

"Well, come in! Come in! Can't see you out there," her grandmother said.

"Look, Kerry,—Mr. Kendall, I don't think—" Mark began.

"She won't be content now until she sees you," Mr. Kendall laughed. "Come on."

"Who is this young man, Kerry? Your beau?" the elder Mrs. Kendall inquired as they entered the bedroom.

Kerry blushed. "Grandma, this is Mark Lee."

"Mark Lee, did you say? Know his mother. One of the Fenton girls, isn't she? Married that Lee fellow. Justin Lee, wasn't it? Died a few years ago. Mother's a music teacher."

Kerry was dumbfounded. Grandma catalogued the facts about Mark as though she were reading them from a book. And I didn't know anything about him.

"That's right, Mrs. Kendall." Mark was completely at ease. "I guess you know all the old families in Winston."

"Know them and buried half of them," she answered drily. "Here, come sit here—on the bed," she invited.

Mark sat at the foot of the bed. Puzzled, Kerry stared at her mother and father. What were they thinking? Neither of them looked too surprised; they were both smiling. Neither of them seemed to see anything unusual in her grandmother's welcoming Mark, a perfect stranger, so warmly.

"What happened to your father, Mark? Died in an accident, wasn't it?" the elder Mrs. Kendall persisted.

I wish she wouldn't say that, Kerry worried. Mark might not like her being so inquisitive.

But he didn't seem to mind. "Yes, Mrs. Kendall. He was killed in an automobile accident. Some high school kids had— had been drinking and they plowed into his car."

No wonder he insisted he never drives with one hand, thought Kerry. But I wish she wouldn't interrogate him any more.

Obviously Mr. Kendall was in agreement. "Mother," he said, "Mrs. Stark, Dr. Stark's wife, is interested in buying some of the furniture. Or, at least, in looking at it."

"Getting rid of my things before my body is cold, eh?" she asked querulously.

"Now, Mother! You know what the doctor said. You have to give up this big old place."

"You know what the doctor said. You have to give up this big old place," she mimicked.

The front door bell rang and Mr. Kendall went down to answer it.

"I don't care who *that* is!" snapped Miss Ashley, the stern-visaged, grey-haired day nurse. "No more visitors!" She got up from her chair and proceeded to herd Kerry and Mark out the door. "And you two can wait downstairs."

"Yes," agreed Kerry's mother. "You and Mark help Dad. Grandma and I have things to talk about," she said firmly.

The elder Mrs. Kendall sniffed.

"That will be some conversation," laughed Kerry on the way downstairs. "You know who will do all the talking. Grandma!"

"She's quite a gal!" Mark declared.

Andrea and her mother were in the living room with Mr. Kendall. Mrs. Stark, her face flushed with excitement, was exclaiming over each chair, each table. She caressed them lovingly.

Andrea beckoned Kerry and Mark to follow her out into the hall.

"I've never seen her so—so all shook up," whispered Andrea. "What did I tell you? She loves all this old stuff. She'd probably like to buy the place, as is!"

"Who wouldn't?" Mark said. "This is a real house, not like those—those ugly little identical boxes that chase each other up and down the streets in the developments outside of town."

"I don't go for those either," agreed Andrea, "but I wouldn't want to live in this morgue!"

"Andrea!" Kerry cried.

"Sorry, chum, but that's how I feel. Just give me a tent on the dunes or a shack in the woods."

"You and Thoreau," commented Mark, drily.

"Now, look here, Mark, you told me once that you were going to spend your summers on Cape Cod—when you were in college. You said that you'd be able to write there—with nothing but sea and sky and sand—"

"That's right," he interrupted. "But I'm speaking of a home—when you are married and have a family."

"Well, you'd have to have a lot of kids to fill up a place like this," she giggled, nudging Kerry.

He is different, Kerry realized. Most boys his age don't think much beyond tomorrow. I haven't, either. I never thought of marriage, beyond the wedding. And I never considered children—until now. I would like to have Mark's children. I'll have half a dozen, she decided fiercely. Being an only child is lonesome.

"Andrea," Mrs. Stark announced as she and Mr. Kendall came out of the library, "we're leaving now. Mr. Kendall and the young man are going to deliver a couch and some chairs this afternoon," she said happily, her eyes sparkling.

"Kerry," her mother called softly over the bannister. "I will be down in a minute. Grandma is asleep. Tell Dad I am ready to go."

"But he and Mark are going to deliver the couch and chairs to Mrs. Stark's first," she answered.

"I will drive you and your mother home," Mrs. Stark offered.

Mrs. Kendall demurred, but Andrea's mother insisted. When

they reached Kerry's house, her mother invited them to stay for supper so the two women settled themselves in the living room, and Kerry and Andrea went upstairs.

"How frou-frou!" Andrea commented as she stood in the doorway of Kerry's bedroom.

"I like it!" Kerry protested.

"I guess I do, too," Andrea agreed grudgingly. "For you, that is. It is certainly female. And I like this," she said, pointing to the fireplace. "I would like a fireplace in my room. I could lie in front of it and think long, long thoughts."

"Want a fire?" Kerry asked.

"Sure."

Kerry opened the low maple chest by the fireplace and took out some logs. In a few minutes, a small fire was coiling up the chimney. They sat silently, watching the shadows flicker on the walls. The constant hum of conversation drifted up from the living room.

"Sybil and your mother certainly hit it off," Andrea murmured dreamily as she gazed into the flames.

"I noticed that. They haven't stopped talking since we got home."

After supper, Mrs. Stark, over Mrs. Kendall's and Kerry's protests, washed the dishes. Then she and Andrea left, but not before she had made Kerry's mother promise to come to visit her.

When Mark left, Kerry went to the door with him.

"Thanks for giving up a Sunday afternoon to help Dad," she said.

"I enjoyed it. And I got to see you," he reminded her, taking her hand.

"I know, Mark," she smiled up at him.

"Kerry, you don't have a date for the Football Frolic, do you?"

"No, not yet."

"Will you go with me?"

"You know I will!"

"Good. It's not 'til just before Thanksgiving so we will have lots of time to talk about it. But I wanted to make sure that you wouldn't go with anyone else." He squeezed her hand. "I'd better say good-night, Kerry."

After he had left, she raced into the living room.

"Mom! I'm going to the Football Frolic!"

"Are you?" her mother smiled. "And when is it?"

"Not 'til Thanksgiving. It is a formal. Do you think I could get a new gown?"

"I guess so. Financially, things are going to be a lot easier now, you know."

Kerry looked at both her parents puzzled.

"Grandma insists upon paying us board when she comes to live here," her mother continued. "I was just telling Dad. She and I had a long conversation this afternoon. I told her we wouldn't think of it, but she insists."

"I think it's because it will make her more independent," Mr. Kendall commented.

"She's—she's—a lot different," Kerry said hesitantly.

"She's frightened. She has always been self-sufficient, but now, she knows she has to rely upon others. And I think she is relieved, in a way. I often used to think she wasn't completely happy, living there alone. I think she would have liked to come to live with us," her father explained.

Kerry and her mother exchanged glances.

"And now she is," Mrs. Kendall said. "And we are going to make it as pleasant as we can. I am really going to enjoy having her."

Mr. Kendall leaned forward in his chair, took his wife's hand and said earnestly, "Thank you, Kit." Then he got up, bent down and kissed her.

Kerry laughed, "I'll leave you two love-birds. I have to shampoo my hair."

As she left the room, she turned. Her father was sitting next to her mother, her head on his shoulder. At their age, grinned Kerry. Still in love! I hope that, after twenty years, my husband and I still feel that way. My husband? Mark?

CHAPTER XIV

The following weeks skittered by magically. At home, everything ran smoothly. Grandma Kendall was happy and most agreeable. The doctor instructed her to take her pills and resume normal existence, so she insisted upon helping with the housework and in preparing meals. She had changed completely. She talked long hours with Kerry's mother, and there was never even the slightest disagreement. One evening, for dinner, she made a lemon meringue pie. Its delicate, flaky crust and mouth-watering filling were topped with towering snowy mounds, lightly browned. When Kerry's mother complimented her, she hushed her and confided that she considered her daughter-in-law's lemon meringue pie far superior to hers.

When Grandma first walked into the spare room, she stopped

and caught her breath. Kerry and her mother had furnished it with pieces from the old house, a mahogany wash stand with its white ironstone pitcher and bowl that Kerry had filled with roses from the Sanford's greenhouse, a rocking chair upholstered in pale blue satin. On the walls were old flower prints from the other house, framed in time-worn gold. The younger Mrs. Kendall had covered the headboard of Kerry's twin bed with blue satin to match the chair. Even the white candlewick spread was a family heirloom. The only addition was the soft blue rug bordered with pink roses.

"Why this looks like home!" Grandma exclaimed. "And roses! How did you know I love them? They are my favorite flower."

"I knew," Kerry answered. "When I was little, I always remember your dresser drawers smelled of roses. Was it a sachet, Grandma?"

"Pot-pourri, Kerry. I will show you how to make it."

And she did, with the petals from the bouquets which Mr. Kendall brought from the greenhouse each week.

The only time she was irascible was when she discovered that her home was going to be torn down to make way for an apartment house. She balked, at first, at selling it, until her son convinced her that there was no other solution.

Mark was disturbed, too. "Eventually," he remarked morosely, "this will be a county of apartments, developments, supermarkets, and super-highways." He even wrote an editorial about it for the school paper.

He was surprised and delighted when Grandma Kendall invited him to choose, before the antique dealer arrived, whatever books he wanted from her library. He eagerly packed carton after carton. Kerry remonstrated, wondering where he was going to put them, but he assured her that he would find space. One afternoon he invited her to see for herself.

She was a little frightened at the prospect of meeting Mrs. Lee, and tried on four dresses before she was satisfied with her appearance.

Grandma Kendall teased, "Don't worry, Kerry. All mothers-in-law are not like me!"

Mrs. Lee was in the kitchen when Mark opened the door and shouted, "Mom! I'm home! I brought you a visitor."

His mother came into the living room, patting her hair and smoothing her apron.

Why, she is as nervous as I am, realized Kerry.

She was a tall woman; soft black hair accentuated her thin white face and enormous dark eyes.

They look so much alike, Kerry thought. Mark is a carbon copy of his mother.

"Mom, this is Kerry," Mark said. "My best girl friend."

"Hello, Kerry. I am glad to see you at last. Mark has told me about you constantly." She smiled warmly.

"Hello, Mrs. Lee," Kerry said.

"Now that you two have met, I'll show Kerry where I put all those books she was sure I wouldn't have room for," Mark said.

"Mark is very grateful for your grandmother's thoughtfulness," Mrs. Lee remarked. "Books, any books, are his life, as you probably know by now."

"You two can talk at dinner. Come on, Kerry," he urged.

"At dinner? But, Mark, I didn't plan to—"

"Oh, I forgot! I told your mother you were going to stay, but I didn't tell you," he grinned.

"Mark! You didn't! I told you to ask Kerry this morning," Mrs. Lee chided.

"I know. I'm sorry," he apologized. "Forgive me, Kerry?" He took her hand.

Embarrassed, Kerry nodded. What would his mother think about hand-holding in front of her? I want her to like me! She attempted to withdraw her hand but Mark held it tight.

"Mother doesn't mind my holding hands with my best girl," he teased, reading her thoughts.

Mrs. Lee laughed. "It's about time!" She winked at Kerry and returned to the kitchen.

She does like me, Kerry decided happily. It's a good thing, too, because she and Mark are very close. Like Dad and Grandma. But not exactly like Dad and Grandma, she hoped fervently.

Although the Lee cottage was small, Mark's room was spacious. One whole wall was covered with bookshelves, from floor to ceiling. Books lay, stood upright, and leaned—on the shelves, on his desk, on his window sill.

"See? I told you I would have lots of room," he pointed out.

"It's a wonder you don't have them in your closet," Kerry said.

"I do," he said, opening the door.

The top closet shelf was piled high with notebooks. "These are originals," he boasted. "These are the books I have written."

"That you have written?"

"Sure. I started when I was in elementary school. The first

one was a thriller, *The Black Widow Mystery!* Wrote it when I was nine. Some day," he promised, "I will let you read it! I will let you read all of them."

After dinner, Mrs. Lee sat and talked with them. Self-conscious at first, eventually Kerry found herself chatting freely with Mark's mother. She is so warm and natural, so interested, Kerry thought. She must be a good teacher.

When Kerry told Mrs. Lee about her plans for studying horticulture, the latter asked, "Had you ever thought about teaching?"

"No, not really," Kerry admitted. "I think I want to be a—I think I want to do research. Or maybe landscape architecture. I am not sure."

"Landscape architecture! That is a long grind, especially for a girl," Mrs. Lee said. "You know, teaching is a practical profession for a woman, Kerry. It is good insurance. If you get married, you can always go back to it—if you have to," she said quietly.

"Anyone that marries me will have to slave and earn money to support me while I am writing the great American novel," Mark joked.

"I am sure of that," Mrs. Lee laughed as she got up. She patted Kerry's shoulder. "Come in and say good-night when you go, Kerry."

The evening flew by. They talked about everything, especially about school. Strange, thought Kerry, I never run out of things to say to Mark. It is as though I had known him forever. I can tell him my secrets, my dreams; I can't do that even with my mother or with Andrea, my best friend.

At ten o'clock, she went in to say good-night to Mrs. Lee and to thank her. Mark's mother made her promise to come very soon again.

When they reached home, Mark parked the car outside the gate and walked to the door with Kerry. She peered up at him in the dim light that shone through the window. He bent down and brushed his lips against her forehead.

"Good-night, best girl friend," he murmured. "See you in school tomorrow." And he ran down the driveway.

Perplexed, Kerry stood for a moment, her hand on the door knob. What is it, she wondered. What is it inside him that makes him aloof with me? I don't expect passionate love scenes; I wouldn't like that. But, since that first day, he has held me at arm's length. And I want him to hold me in his arms. I wish I could talk to Mother about it, about how I feel. But I can't. What would she think of me?

The next few weeks were halcyon ones. Kerry was happier than she had ever been in her life. Since she had swimming practice once a week and Runes meeting twice a week, Mark offered to drive her home every day. It was a relief not to have to endure the long bus ride home, cooped up with the boisterous junior high students. After they left school each day, she and Mark would stroll slowly down to the Hut for a Coke.

It was a glorious fall. Day after perfect day, a golden, gleaming sun swung across a dazzling blue sky. The mornings sparkled; the evenings glowed with the luminous turquoise and the lush lilac of sunset. The stinging smell of leaves burning spiced the transparent clarity of the air.

Sometimes she and Mark would scuffle through the faded

yellow and brown leaves that lined the gutters; other times, hurdle the piles that some tidy homeowner had raked into a heap. And they always wound up finally, intoxicated with just being alive, at the same table in the same corner in the Hut. The other students never occupied their place; it seemed an unwritten law that it belonged to Mark and Kerry. The Crew seldom frequented the Hut that late in the afternoon; they usually stopped in immediately after school and then raced off in their cars to "greener fields," as Mark put it. If an occasional Crew member did stop for a soda or a Coke, they spoke to both Mark and Kerry. Except for Tracey. She always greeted Mark sweetly but ignored Kerry. But Kerry was oblivious; Tracey was from another life, one past and almost completely forgotten. It was Mark and Kerry now. She felt sorry for the other girl, sorry that Tracey, like a dog in a manger, couldn't let go of a boy who no longer cared for her.

Only one small event marred the otherwise idyllic existence. It was a minor incident that occurred in Mr. Ford's history class and both Mark and Andrea insisted that it was unimportant. But it bothered Kerry because she didn't want anything to scratch the flawless, shining surface of her days.

One Friday Mr. Ford was lecturing in his usual cannonading tones. His voice boomed, swelled, and crashed futilely against the deaf, last-day-of-the-week ears of the seniors who lounged, sprawled or slumped in their seats. Only Kerry and Kenneth Sanford listened; Kerry, because she found the teacher interesting; Kenneth, for other reasons. Ever since the first day when Mr. Ford had made the sarcastic remarks about Kenneth's having come from a private school, the boy had sat, stiff and sternly critical, noting every word of every lecture. Several times he had caustically questioned the instructor about the latter's opinions. A few times Kenneth had been overtly rude, but Mr. Ford had back-handed the boy's remarks and made him look foolish in the eyes of his classmates.

On this particular day, the teacher was discussing capitalism. He had outlined its origins, its purposes and its future. A few students, like automatons, lackadaisically jotted down random notes. The others doodled or gazed out of the window.

"Capitalism is a kind of financial fascism!" Mr. Ford shouted. "The few feed upon the many!"

"That is treason!" Kenneth shouted suddenly. "You are a Communist, a lousy Communist!"

The students woke up and sat up, stunned. The teacher strode over to Kenneth and observed, "Well, at least you are listening, Sanford. What's your beef? Financial fascism. Think about it."

"Think about it yourself! I am not sitting here and listening to any more of your Red propaganda, Ford!" The boy lurched out of his seat and out of the classroom.

"Sanford! Come back and sit down!" the teacher ordered. Ignoring him, Kenneth continued down the hall.

"One of you guys tell him I want to see him after school," he announced.

Kenny had a right to say that, Kerry thought angrily. Ford had done nothing but belittle him since that first day. The boy is arrogant, and I don't like him particularly, but he doesn't deserve the treatment he has been getting in this class. And then, without thinking, she blurted out, "Mr. Ford, I don't think you are very fair to him!" When she realized what she had said, she stared, horrified, at the teacher.

The other students swung around and gazed at her incredulously. They were even more surprised at her outburst than they had been at Kenneth's. Mr. Ford was, too!

"Well, Kerry, what prompted this defense?" he snapped. "It isn't spring, so it can't be love."

The class hooted. Kerry frowned. They are not laughing because of his remark, she thought. They are amused at the utterly ridiculous possibility of my aspiring to Kenneth Sanford, the big man on campus and a Crew leader. But I don't care! I don't care what they think! I mean it.

"Now you are trying to embarrass me," she accused. "Just the way you have embarrassed Kenneth."

"Kerry," he ordered, "come in after school and discuss this. You are wasting class time." And he continued his lecture.

Why did I do it? She knew. Ford had pushed the boy outside the pale, had made him appear different, that first day. He had implied that Kenny thought he was superior because he had been to prep school. And no one likes to be a maverick, especially a high school student, Kerry thought. We want to be just like everyone else. We want to be "in." I defended Kenny because "There, but for the grace of God, go I."

When the bell rang, she gathered up her books and hurried out, hoping to see Mark in the corridor before her next class. She wanted, needed, his approbation. As she reached the door, Bob Ramsay came up behind her and poked her gently in the back.

"Atta girl!" he whispered. "I guess you told him!"

She turned and gawked at him. This was the first time that any one of the Crew had deigned to speak to her directly! Before she could recover, Merry Raleigh, who was directly behind Bob, leaned over and murmured, "Good for you, Kerry!"

Before she could reply, she was swept out of the room and down the hall by the throng of students. She failed to see Mark until after school. She had time only to tell him that she had an appointment with the history teacher and to ask him to wait for her.

When she reached Mr. Ford's room, Kenneth was already there, slumped sideway in a seat, his long legs stretched out into the aisle. The teacher was checking homework papers. As Kerry hesitated in the doorway, he looked up.

"Come in and sit down," he directed. "I will be with you in a minute."

Kerry slid into a seat. She glanced hesitantly at the boy, but he ignored her completely, his eyes riveted on a portrait of Washington that hung over the blackboard behind the teacher's desk.

"Well? What have you to say for yourself, Sanford?" Mr. Ford asked, pushing his chair back from the desk and hooking his hands in his belt.

"Nothing." The boy continued to inspect the picture.

"Let me tell you something, Sanford," the teacher began. "You are one of the few people in this class who have any idea what I have been talking about since September. You and Kerry here. And I appreciate that. Most of these boobs don't care; it's just a class, another class to be endured. I know that.

I admit that American history and world problems probably seem pretty remote from the things that really interest you at this stage—at this time of your life. Oh, we teachers like to think that every pearl we drop before you is picked up and fondled and stored away. But you and I know it doesn't happen that way, don't we? I just try to keep you awake. That's why I do some of the things I do—some of the kookie things. You two ought to know that; you are intelligent enough." He leaned forward and peered at Kenneth and then at Kerry.

I never realized before why he acted the way he does, Kerry thought. The slang he uses in class, the nicknames he has for the kids, the derisive terms he applies to things he doesn't approve of. She recalled the time he had described the designers of suburban developments as "architectual illiterates." And television commercials as "electronic garbage." When she had told Mark, he had laughed and said that what education needed was more egg-heads like Ford, instead of the typical instructor who digested the text-book, spoon-fed it to his students and expected them to "regurgitate it" as he put it, on a test.

"I can see that you know what I am talking about, Kerry," Mr. Ford said, "even though our mutual friend here doesn't, or won't try." He stood up. "You may go, Kerry. Next time, when you feel that you have to spring to the defense of the underdog, keep it under your wig until after school, will you? Bull Durham wouldn't like such a breach of discipline, you know. Must have discipline!" he barked, pulling in his stomach, expanding his chest and clicking his heels in a mock military posture.

Kerry grinned. "Yes, sir!" she snapped out and saluted.

The teacher laughed and walked to the door with her. "See you tomorrow," he said.

Kerry corrected him. "Not tomorrow. Monday."

"That's right. You see, I love this job so much that I had forgotten it was Friday," he mocked, as he closed the door after her.

She hurried down the hall to where Mark was waiting. She told him the whole story over a Coke at the Hut. He simply nodded and said, "Ford is all right. He is a good teacher, but most of those numbskulls don't appreciate him."

"Do you think I was wrong?" Kerry said.

"Frankly, yes. Nobody has the right to criticize a teacher in class. You and Sanford were doing the same thing that you dislike Ford for. You were trying to make him look inadequate in front of his students."

"I know," Kerry agreed.

"Listen, teachers have it rough enough without wise guys like Kenny—"

"And like me?" she teased.

"Yes, like you," he grinned, leaning across the table and lacing his fingers through hers. "Now let's forget it."

And she did. She never heard what happened after she had left the room that Friday. And she didn't really care. The incident dropped like a tiny pebble into the placid pool of her existence, causing scarcely a ripple.

CHAPTER XV

The Saturday before the Football Frolic Kerry and her mother planned to drive into town to buy a gown for the dance. That morning, as they waited in the driveway for her father to bring Old Faithful to the house, a car came slowly down the drive from the direction of the big house. When it rolled to a stop, Kerry was surprised to see her father at the wheel.

"Did Mr. Sanford lend Dad a car?" she asked.

"No, the bank did," her mother laughed.

"The bank?"

"Dad got a loan from the bank."

"Oh, Mom! Thank goodness! A car! And no more truck!"

"I know what you mean," her mother agreed.

Of course she must have been inconvenienced by the necessity of having to ride in Old Faithful, Kerry realized. But she didn't say a word. My open resentment didn't help any, she thought ruefully.

As they pulled into the parking lot next to the dress shop, Andrea and her mother were getting into their car.

"Kerry! Hi! Buying a gown?"

"Yes," Kerry answered, running over to the Stark car. I feel guilty, she realized. Andrea doesn't have a date for the dance and I do. Maybe Mark could ask someone to take her. No! Andrea wouldn't like that. She would jeer at that suggestion.

"Wait 'til you see the little number I bought," Andrea boasted.

"For the—for the Frolic?" Kerry stammered.

"Why not, chum? I am not an old maid yet."

Mrs. Stark protested, "Andrea! Didn't you tell Kerry?"

"Nope. Wanted to save it for a surprise," Andrea explained.

"Tell me what? Tell me what? Andrea!" Kerry asked.

"I have a date for the dance," Andrea announced smugly. "A dream boat, if I must say so myself."

"Who? Who is it?" Kerry persisted.

"It is a boy I used to know in New York years ago. He was a little stinker, a real goon. But now! He has grown up into— but you will have to wait until Friday night," she concluded.

"Why didn't you tell me before?" Kerry insisted. "Here I have been worrying about your not having a date."

"To tell the truth, chum, I didn't know myself until last night," confessed Andrea. "Jamie and his mother were on their way back to the city and they stopped in to see us."

"But what's he like?"

"You'll see. Friday night."

"Come, Kerry. We have to get going," her mother said.

Andrea rolled up the window of the car and pretended to swoon as they drove away.

"Oh, that girl!" exclaimed Kerry. "What's the big secret? She won't even tell me what her date looks like!"

"That is her privilege. You don't tell her everything, do you?"

"No, but this is different. I wonder what kind of gown she bought," Kerry said as they went into the shop.

"She probably won't tell you that, either," her mother laughed. "She will tell you to wait until Friday night."

Kerry tried on several dresses, but she didn't see one that she really liked. It has to be perfect, she decided. This would be the first time that Mark would see her in a formal and she wanted it to be the most beautiful gown ever created. When the salesgirl finally informed her that there were no more in her size, Mrs. Kendall suggested that they try another store.

"But wait!" the salesgirl said. "There *is* another one. It's a little more expensive—and a wee bit older than these—"

"Look at it, Kerry," her mother suggested. "If you like it, I don't think Dad will mind the price. It is your first formal at Winston High, and you can always use it next year when you go to college."

It was the most stunning gown Kerry had ever seen in her life. As it slid smoothly over her head and shoulders she knew how she would look in it. And she was right. It had been made especially for her. The bronze velvet strapless bodice clung to her and made her still faintly-tanned skin glow. The warm color deepened the soft topaz of her eyes and accented her honey-streaked hair.

"Oh, Mom," she breathed ecstatically. "Isn't it perfect?"

"It is lovely," her mother admitted. "But it does seem a—a little too sophisticated for a high school dance."

"Mom! It isn't! Seniors don't wear those—those things you wore when you were in high school!"

Mrs. Kendall and the saleslady exchanged amused glances.

"And besides," she said, "I can wear it next year at college. You said so yourself. If I got one of those kid dresses, I wouldn't be able to wear it at State—at college."

"All right," her mother agreed reluctantly. "If you like it, we'll take it."

"You can buy white shoes in the bridal shop on the third floor and have them dyed to match," the clerk suggested.

Kerry found a pair of heels in the bridal shop to fit her, and the salesman promised faithfully that he could dye them and have them ready on Thursday.

The next week dragged its feet. Classes were interminable; each day was an eternity. By Thursday, Kerry was counting the hours.

Friday night she was ready a half hour before Mark came. When she walked into the living room, Grandma frowned at her.

"Looks a little old for a high school girl," she snapped.

"Oh, Grandma! It isn't like when you were a girl. Everybody wears gowns like this now!"

"It isn't even like when I was a girl," her mother commented wryly. "Or so I was told."

"Mom! You *said* you liked it."

"I do. And Grandma will, too. It just needs getting used to." Mrs. Kendall winked slowly at her mother-in-law.

"Needs something to take away that bare look," Grandma decided. "Go up to my room. In my dresser, there is a jewel box. Bring it here."

When Grandma opened the box, she took out some topaz earrings. They glittered like the tawny rays of a clear, sparkling sunset.

"Here. Put them on," she directed.

Kerry held them in her hand. "They are beautiful!"

"Match your eyes," Grandma commented. "Here, put this on, too." She handed Kerry a slim, delicate bracelet, set with tiny winking topazes.

"It's perfect!" exclaimed Kerry, sliding it on her arm.

Isn't that just like Grandma, Kerry mused. As though jewelry would make me look less undressed! But it did, she realized, as she looked into the hall mirror. It was the final touch.

When Mark came, he obviously agreed. "You look like a model," he said, "too glamorous for a high school dance."

"You don't think I'm too—that the dress is too formal?" She was worried.

"No. Wait 'til you see some of the—the way some of them dress!"

"It puzzles me," said Grandma.

"What puzzles you?" Mrs. Kendall asked.

"Where she is going to put that!" Grandma pointed to the florist's box that Mark was carrying.

"Don't worry, Grandma Kendall," he assured her. "The girls already have taken care of it, since they started wearing their gowns at half-mast. The florist explained it to me. They wear wrist corsages." He handed the box to Kerry.

The corsage was a delicate brown and beige cymbidium orchid; it trembled like a huge butterfly on Kerry's wrist.

"It is perfect, Mark. Thank you," she said breathlessly.

"By the way, where are you going after the dance, Mark?" Mr. Kendall asked.

"To the Cabin, sir. They have a juke box for dancing. All the high school kids go there after dances and games. Don't worry, sir. He doesn't serve liquor to students. He has two boys of his own at Winston High."

"You mean he refuses to serve high school students?" asked Mr. Kendall.

"Yes," Mark answered. "That is why some of the crowd doesn't go there."

The Crew, Kerry thought. She had heard that some of the girls as well as the boys drank now and then, to show off.

"We will be home by two o'clock, if that is all right with you, sir," Mark assured them. "Or is that too late?"

"Between 1:30 and 2," suggested Mrs. Kendall.

On the way to the dance, Kerry apologized to Mark. "I am sorry, Mark, but Grandma is a little old-fashioned."

"Why shouldn't she be? She is just remembering when life

was slower and more graceful and women—girls—were something to be cherished."

"And we are not now?" Kerry teased.

"Hardly!" Mark heckled. "Not when you have equal rights with men. *You* should be protecting *us!*"

"That could be arranged. I think I might be capable of protecting you," she answered boldly. "I may be supporting you, anyway."

Mark was silent. She glanced at him. The faint light from the dashboard sketched grim shadows on his lean face. Did I go too far, she wondered unhappily. Maybe I shouldn't have said that. Maybe I had better talk about something else.

"Mark?"

"Hm?"

"What is the theme of the Frolic? Have you seen the decorations?"

"No. I haven't. The Crew is running the dance, as usual. They wouldn't even let anyone in the gym today. Sanford is chairman so you can expect something real weird."

When they arrived at the school, there was a long line in the corridor outside the gymnasium. Couples were being directed upstairs to the balcony.

"What is going on?" Kerry asked when Mark had returned from the cloakroom.

"Who knows? Maybe we all have to jump from the balcony. Got a parachute?" he grinned.

He wasn't far from wrong. When they finally reached the top of the stairs, they stopped short. A long metal slide, similar to the kind used at pools and lakes in the summer, was propped up against the balcony. Couples had to climb to the top of the apparatus, sit down and slide down to the floor below.

"Oh, Mark, I can't!" Kerry wailed. "I will ruin my dress!"

"What a stupid idea for a formal," Mark said disapprovingly. "For a record dance, it would be kind of fun, but tonight! Look, if you really don't want to go down that silly thing, we will go out to the Cabin now and have something to eat and forget the Frolic."

Kerry watched frantically as the other couples went shooting down the slide. The girls giggled and shrieked, but not one of them refused to take her turn. I have to do it, Kerry realized. Somehow I *have* to do it!

"I will be all right," she assured him. "It was just sort of a shock, that's all."

When it was their turn, she climbed uncertainly to the top of the slide and sat down gingerly, clutching the sides. Neil Maxon, his huge bulk encased in a tuxedo, leaned over her.

"Don't hang on, doll. You'll burn the skin right off those gorgeous hands." He placed both of his big hands around her waist and bent close.

"I don't need any help, thanks," Kerry said coldly, turning to glare at him.

His fat, perspiring face was only inches away from hers and she could smell the nauseating odor of stale beer. She jerked away from him, held her skirt with both hands and pushed with both heels. She shot down the slide into the waiting arms of Kenneth Sanford who stood on a gym mat at the bottom.

He helped her to her feet and she started to step away. But he didn't let go. He kept his arms around her so that she was unable to move. He didn't say a word; he just stared, the same insolent curve on his lips. Kerry couldn't free herself. She didn't want to. What's the matter with me, she asked herself furiously. I am in love with Mark, but this boy excites me. I can't see or hear anything, except Kenneth. It is as though the dancers, the orchestra, the lights had all disappeared and we two are alone. And he knows it, too, she realized angrily.

Suddenly a raucous voice shattered the silence between them. "Hey, Sanford! Break it up!" shouted Neil from the balcony. "Save that for Poplar Pond! There's a lot of customers waiting up here!"

Wordlessly, Kenneth let go of her, so abruptly that she stumbled and almost fell. He made no effort to help her; he didn't apologize. He simply returned to his place at the base of the slide.

Mark came next flying down and he landed upright, unassisted. Without a word, he swung her out on the floor. Neither of them spoke. What is he thinking, Kerry wondered. Did he see? Does he know? She turned her head from his shoulder and glanced up at him. But his face was impassive, blank, as usual. If I only had his poker face, she wished.

"Something?" he asked, smiling down at her.

"No. I was just going to say—" she fumbled. What *am* I going to say? What is he going to say?

"You were just going to say?"

"That the decorations are something. They are really something, aren't they? Where do you suppose they found all those animals? And the toys? Where do you suppose they got all those toys?" she babbled.

"I didn't think you noticed," he said. "Yes, the decorations are clever."

The gymnasium had been transformed into an enormous playroom, a child's nursery. Stuffed tigers, lions and pandas pursued each other around the walls; plush monkeys, dangling from the baskets, leered down at the dancers. Toy wagons chauffered by dolls, large and small, angled out from the corners. Gigantic plastic lollipops fenced in the orchestra. From the ceiling hundreds of model airplanes floated over the heads of the crowd.

When the music stopped, they threaded their way through the throng to a table in the corner near the band. Nursery lamps, with music boxes in their bases, tinkled in the center of each table. As Kerry reached out to wind up their music box, she felt someone nudge her with an elbow.

"Hi, chum." It was Andrea, in a bouffant black gown that made her look slim and tall. Her hair had been tinted a silvery blonde; her lipstick was a pastel pink. She doesn't look brittle any more, Kerry marveled. Why, this is the way her mother must have looked when she was young! Soft and feminine.

"Andrea! What a difference! You look really beautiful!" Kerry exclaimed.

"Thanks, chum. This is the real me, the color of my hair, I mean," she explained, patting her head. "You like?" Without waiting for an answer, she said, "This is Jamie. Kerry and Mark, Jamie."

He was tall, taller than Mark. His flaming red hair made him stand out, like a beacon, above the heads of the other students. Myriads of freckles, like minute copper coins, dappled his strong, square face.

After the introductions, the next number started, and Andrea suggested they exchange partners. Kerry enjoyed the next few minutes.

Jamie was a smooth dancer and an entertaining conversationalist. She found out that he wanted to be a psychologist and was even contemplating enrolling at Dr. Stark's alma mater. And he liked Andrea, principally he said, because she was so sincere and honest. He had dated other girls, he confessed, but he had not met one he wanted to go steady with until he met Andrea.

"A guy knows where he stands with her," he explained. "She lets you know just how she feels about you. About everything."

"I know, Jamie. That's why I like—"

She stopped in the middle of a sentence. Kenneth Sanford had just tapped Jamie on the shoulder. Jamie smiled, stepped back and walked to the side of the gymnasium. Without a word, Kenneth swung her down the floor. She didn't know what to say to this sphinx. And he gave her no encouragement. He simply held her close, almost too close. But he was the best partner she had ever danced with. She found herself doing intricate steps she had never dreamed of doing. Soon there were whispers and side glances from the Crew. She didn't know whether they were triggered by Kenneth's dancing with someone outside the pale or by their admiration for the dexterity that she and Kenneth were displaying. Soon they were the center of attraction. Kerry didn't care. She was breathless at the nearness of this boy. She closed her eyes and abandoned herself to the music.

Suddenly he stopped. She opened her eyes. Tiger Torrance had tapped Kenneth on the shoulder. Kenny looked at her for a moment without uttering a word, turned and lost himself in the crowd. Tiger complimented her on her dress and then blurted out his admiration for her defense of Kenneth in history class. Before she could answer, another and another boy cut in, all members of the Crew. They all made a point to mention the incident in Ford's class. Dazed, she was whirled from one to another.

At the intermission, her partner took her over to Mark who was standing near the stag line with Andrea and Jamie.

"Mark, I'm sorry," she began. "I don't understand it—all those boys dancing with me. Most of them never even spoke to me before!"

"Welcome, belle of the ball," Andrea grinned. "What gives?"

"I don't know, Andrea. Honestly, I don't!" she protested.

"Sanford's idea, probably," said Mark. "He gave orders and they fell in line."

"But, why, Mark? He didn't say one word to me all the time we were dancing!"

"That didn't seem to bother you," Mark commented. "You seemed to be enjoying yourself."

"He is a good dancer," she said. "Is there anything wrong with—"

"Hey, you two. Where are you going after this brawl?" interrupted Andrea.

Thank you, Andrea, Kerry breathed silently. Thank you for averting what might have turned into a quarrel.

"To the Cabin," Mark answered. "Want to come?" He seemed to have forgotten that he and Kerry had been on the verge of an argument.

During the rest of the evening, Mark refused to permit any-one to cut in, and, after the first few rebuffs, the stag line gave up. Mark's anger, if it had been anger, seemed to have evaporated. At the Cabin after the dance, he and Jamie discussed everything from the World Series to College Boards.

At one o'clock Mark announced that he and Kerry had to leave.

"At one o'clock! You don't have a one o'clock curfew, do you?" Andrea asked.

"No! Mark! Mom said—"

"We are leaving," Mark said curtly.

While the boys were getting their cars, Kerry confided to Andrea, "I never know what he is going to do. My mother told me to be home between half-past one and two!"

"I told you about Mark. If you really like him, you will just have to grin and bear it. Maybe he thinks he is punishing you for your frolicking at the Frolic," Andrea laughed.

"But it wasn't my fault! I didn't *ask* those boys to dance with me!"

"Come on," called Jamie.

Andrea ran over to the car. "I'll call you tomorrow—I mean today—and maybe we can do something, the four of us, this week-end."

On the way home, Kerry sat stiffly next to the door, as far

away from Mark as possible. Across a somber night sky, a cold November moon played tag with black cloud-billows. Kerry shivered.

"Better put your arms through the sleeves of that coat," Mark said. "You will catch cold."

Suddenly Kerry was aware that they were on a strange road.

"Mark! Where are we going? This isn't the way home."

"I know."

"Mark! Take me home," she ordered. She was frightened. Andrea was right. No one could ever tell what Mark was thinking, or what he was going to do next.

"Mark! Did you hear me? I want to go home! Now!"

"Eventually."

"Mark! If you don't take me home, I'll—I'll jump out," she threatened, grabbing the door handle.

"Grow up, Kerry. I'm not going to abduct you. We are going out to Poplar Pond."

Poplar Pond? Where had she heard that? Then she remembered. Neil Maxon had said, "Save that for Poplar Pond."

"What's Poplar Pond?"

"It's up on the heights near the country club. It has several appellations—Casanova Causeway, Make-Out Mountain," he said mockingly. "The local lover's lane."

"And what am I supposed to gather from that?" she asked coldly.

"Oh, don't expect a passionate love scene. Not with me."

What does that mean, she puzzled. Is he going to tell me we are through? But why come out here to tell me that?

They turned off the main highway onto a narrow two-lane

road that seemed to have been just newly-surfaced. The shining black ribbon glimmered in the headlights. A few hundred feet ahead there was a foot-wide strip of white paint across the road.

"What is that?" asked Kerry.

"Oh, that is the—I don't know," he answered.

He can't even answer a simple question, Kerry brooded. When she saw a similar strip of paint about a mile beyond, she knew better than to inquire about it.

Mark slowed up and cramped the wheels into the worn ruts of a dirt road. A hundred feet beyond he stopped the car, cut the motor, and dimmed the lights.

"Aren't you going to turn the lights off? Wouldn't that be more romantic?" she asked sarcastically.

"Not on your life. That's the deal with the police. They know high school kids park and they don't mind if they park here. But if they find you with the lights off! Look around. We have company."

When her eyes became accustomed to the dark, Kerry could discern faintly the outlines of two other cars, their pale headlights brushing tree trunks. A brighter light glimmered a few yards in front of their car. It wavered and disappeared and then glistened silver.

"What is that light?" she asked fearfully. I don't like this place, she thought. I wish he would take me home!

"Where? Oh, out there in front of the car? That is moonlight, Kerry. Moonlight on Poplar Pond."

CHAPTER XVI

There was a different note in his voice, a soft, kind tone. Kerry turned to look at him.

"Kerry, come over here. I can't talk to you 'way over there. And that is what I am going to do. Talk. There are a lot of things I want to tell you—a lot of things."

She slid across the seat. He put his arm around her and rubbed his chin on her head as she leaned back.

"But why here, Mark?" she murmured. "Out here in the middle of nowhere?"

"Do you know any other place where we can be alone? Not in school, certainly. At the Hut? At your house or my house? And it is a little too cold to take your best girl for a hike and sit here on a stone wall and talk to her for an hour," he teased.

"Not an hour, Mark," she warned. "I have to be home by two at the latest."

"You will be," he promised.

He was quiet for a few minutes. Through the partially-opened window, she could hear faint music from the other two cars' radios. It sounded lonely and distant. The branches of the dark pines sighed sadly overhead like the slow wash of the sea on a deserted shore. Kerry pulled her coat snugly around her and huddled closer to Mark.

"Cold?" he asked.

"No. It is just that it is so—so still and eerie here." She was torn between her anxiety, to get away from this place, and her desire to hear what Mark was going to tell her. But she didn't know how to tell him.

"Maybe it was foolish, bringing you out here," he admitted. "But I had to talk to you alone. What I'm going to say will determine my whole life—and yours, too, if you agree. So listen, will you, Kerry, and tell me the truth?" he pleaded.

"I promise, Mark," she murmured.

"Remember the first time we met? That Saturday when you were planting bulbs on the front lawn? Did you know that I— I almost kissed you? In broad daylight? And I had only just met you!" He sounded angry.

She smiled in the darkness. She knew.

"I knew then that I was in love with you, a little. And I knew that I was going to fall in love with you, completely and helplessly. It sounds corny, like a movie, but it's true. And I prayed, all the way home that day, that you would feel the same way. I think you do." It wasn't a question; it was a statement.

She tilted her head back and looked up at him. "I do, Mark," she said simply.

"And it has nothing to do with the way you look. It is you, the Kerry inside that I love. Lots of kids get fooled. A boy flips over a girl because she is attractive—has good legs, or—or she's stacked. He rushes her into marriage and then wakes up some day and finds out that he is a bigamist. He has married two girls—the one on the outside and the one on the inside. And he finds out that he has nothing in common with the one on the inside. So they fight. Or they get a divorce," he said bitterly. "Not for me. When I marry, it will be for keeps."

"Mark," she whispered. "What am I like? Inside? What do you think I am like—inside?"

"I know! You are shy and uncertain, sometimes too much so. But that is what I like about you. A man doesn't like a woman who knows everything. He likes to feel that he is—not exactly the boss—but that she will come to him when there are decisions to be made. And that she will respect *his* opinions. It makes a man feel that he is masculine.

"And you are honest, Kerry. Or is it that you are naïve? I can always tell what you are thinking. You never try to conceal things. I like that. I need that, because I am not that way. I keep things bottled up inside and I need someone just the opposite. Can you imagine what our life would be like if you were like me? Two thunder clouds trying to avoid each other, trying to avoid a storm!"

"But what if I became like you? What if I couldn't stand your silence, your moods? Sometimes I worry. I don't know whether I have done something to make you angry—"

"You couldn't be like me. Don't you see? When I am with you, I change. Most of the time, anyway. There is more chance of my becoming like *you*. Ask my mother. She says I am almost human," he laughed. "She says that after we are married, she probably won't recognize me."

He had been discussing their marriage with his mother but he hadn't said anything to me. She was annoyed.

"Mark, you keep talking about our being married, but you —you have never asked me," she blurted out.

"I can't ask you until you have heard what I have to say. Maybe you won't want to," he explained. "I want to write, Kerry. It is half my life; you are the other half. But I need both halves. I want to work on a newspaper in a small town so I can have time to write. And in the beginning, I probably won't make enough for both of us to live on."

"Mark, lots of girls work when they are first married. Sometimes couples get married when they are still in college."

"No! Not for us! We are both going to graduate. If we got married before, you might—we might have children—and you wouldn't be able to finish. And suppose something happened to me? How could you live unless you had a profession, some way to earn a living?"

He is thinking of his mother. And he is right.

"There is something else, Kerry," he continued in a low voice. "You probably have been wondering why I—why I—

haven't tried to make—to make out with you. I have wanted to. I am human. There is nothing wrong with my impulses. But I am afraid."

"Afraid?"

"That we wouldn't be able to stop."

"Mark! What kind of person do you think I am? Don't you think I—do you think I would let you—" She pulled away from him angrily.

"Frankly, I don't know. All I know is that I love you. I love you so much I don't want anything to spoil it. And you love me. Can you honestly say that you would be able to keep your head?"

How can he think that of me? She was hurt deeply. And then she recalled the girls who had been going steady and who left school for an "appendectomy" at some hospital out of town or the ones who went on a "visit" to a relative. Or the ones who left school to get married. She felt sorry for them. She had seen them wheeling baby carriages downtown. And she had seen their husbands in school, subdued, harried, frightened, trying desperately to finish high school and working after school and week-ends to support a family. And some of them had been the "nice" kids, from the best families; others, the "wisest", the most sophisticated.

"No, I can't," she confessed.

"Well, then? Now that you know how I feel, do you think you want to wait? For four years? To be my wife for a hundred and four years?"

"Yes, Mark," she answered happily.

He turned her toward him, put both arms around her and laid his cheek against her. His face was hot. She reached up and touched it. He was perspiring! Then she realized how difficult this had been for him. Outwardly calm and coherent, he must have been torn apart inside. It will be my job, she decided, to help him to resolve all his conflicts from now on, as long as we both shall live. That is what a woman does for a man. That is what marraige is, each one trying to help the other to happiness.

His arms tightened around her and he found her lips. It was a long, slow kiss. She didn't feel pins and needles in her fingers and toes the way she had when Tom had kissed her. This was a warm, safe, secure feeling, as she felt when she curled up on the couch in front of the fire on a bleak, dreary winter day. She clung to him, praying silently, Don't ever let him leave me!

Gently he released her and started the car, explaining, "It is almost 1:30. I had better take you home. Don't want to antagonize my future in-laws."

She sat close to him as he swung the car around and started for the road. Suddenly he stopped and cut the motor.

"What is the matter, Mark?" She sat up.

"Listen!" He pulled the window down.

And then she heard it, too. The sound of voices and car motors down the road.

"What is it?" She was frightened.

"I didn't know they were planning to do it tonight," he said mysteriously.

"Who? Do what?"

"The Crew. You know those white lines on the road. Well, they painted them yesterday. Duke and Ken Sanford are going to have it out tonight."

"Have what out tonight? Mark! What is it?"

"They are going to have a drag race to see who is going to run the gang. The winner will be the leader."

"On this narrow road? Somebody will get hurt."

"Not those two."

"Can we—is there another way out of here, Mark? I don't want to get mixed up in anything like that!"

"You won't be. As soon as they finish, they will take off for some bar to celebrate."

"They sound as if they have already been celebrating. Listen!"

Over the sound of idling motors, they could hear the antiphony of girls' shrieks and masculine shouts. Then there was a sudden lull, followed by the roar of two engines. In a few seconds, to the left through the trees, four headlights stabbed the darkness. Two cars roared down the strip of macadam. One of them was a car-length ahead of the other.

"Can you tell which is which?" Kerry whispered, fascinated in spite of her fear.

"That is Sanford's car, the one in the lead," Mark said, peering through the trees.

The end of his sentence was punctuated by the thunder of the two cars as they rocketed by. A single car followed them at a distance.

"Who is in that car?" Kerry asked.

"Probably Neal Maxon and Tiger. They were to be the judges at the finish line. The rest of the Crew are down the road, waiting to congratulate the winner."

His last words were drowned out by the sudden squealing of tires and a strident, metallic crash that echoed through the woods. There was a silence as though the night had caught its breath; then, a swelling chorus of discordant voices and the counterpoint of rapidly-gunned motors.

"What happened? It sounded as though someone cracked up. Maybe someone was hurt." If anyone is hurt, Kerry thought, the police will be here. We have to get out of here!

"I don't know. I don't think anyone was hurt, or they wouldn't all be leaving."

They could hear the last car scud off into the distance.

He pulled onto the road and turned to the right, explaining, "It is shorter this way. We will be home in five minutes."

And then they saw him. As they rounded a curve, the headlights focused upon a figure sprawled grotesquely at the side of the road like a discarded rag doll.

"Mark! It is Duke!" she cried.

"The fools! The stupid fools! To go away and leave him!" Mark exploded as he stopped the car. "He must have been thrown out when his car hit the fence." He pointed to Duke's convertible which teetered precariously over the brook. The car was undamaged except for a slightly dented hood.

"You are not going to get out, are you, Mark? If my mother knew that I was here!" She clutched his arm frantically.

He turned, his hand on the door handle. "You can't be serious? You mean you want me to leave him lying there?"

"But, Mark, they will be back! Or they will send someone! Let's go!" she pleaded.

"And meanwhile he could die! They left my father like that. If help had reached him in time, he would be alive today!"

"But, Mark, what will I tell my parents?" She was on the verge of tears.

"Tell them the truth!" he barked, running toward Duke.

She sat, frozen, staring at Mark as he bent over the injured boy. He stood up and beckoned to her. But she couldn't move. All she could think of was her parents' reaction. Her mother would be angry. But her father? What would he do?

"Kerry! Come here, will you?" Mark called. "I need your help!"

Stiffly, she slid out of the car and walked slowly toward the two boys.

"Hi, Kerry," Duke said feebly. "You always seem to be around when the Crew needs help."

"Look, Kerry, I know this is a shock," Mark said. "But take it easy. I will explain everything to your parents when we get home. They will understand. I am sure your mother and father wouldn't want you to leave Duke here alone. Trust me, will you?"

Duke looked up at her. "Don't be afraid of me, doll. I can't move. But, if I could!" he jeered.

"Don't be a wise guy, Duke. She is frightened enough as it is," snapped Mark. "I will be right back, Kerry. I am going in to get the ambulance." He put his arm around her. "I will turn Duke's car around and put the headlights on. You can sit in the car. We can't leave him alone. You will stay with him?"

"O.K.," she agreed reluctantly, but her heart thudded as he drove away, after maneuvering Duke's car so that the headlights shone upon the other boy.

"Fine friends you have," Kerry said. "Why did they run off and leave you?"

"It's a long story, doll. Last year a couple of us guys were draggin' and we hit another car. It cost my old man plenty to keep it quiet."

"What do you mean, keep it quiet?"

"Not to let on we were draggin'. We told the cops that we skidded on wet pavement. And the guy we hit—he wasn't sure. Just his car. So my old man's insurance took care of that. And he gave the guy something on the side, not to tell the cops what really happened. But he warned me—if I ever did it again, he would take the car away from me. All the other guys' parents said the same thing. And they meant it!" He shifted his arm and groaned. "Boy! That hurts! I'll bet I've broken my arm. There goes basketball! I would have been varsity this year, too," he boasted.

"But I still don't see why they couldn't have called a doctor," Kerry persisted. "Why did they have to leave you?"

"I told you! If they stayed and the cops came, we would all get tossed into jail. Anyway, they weren't going to leave me here all night. Ken was going to come back for me after he took his date home. I planned to tell them at the hospital that I had decided to take a drive, after I took my girl home, and I just didn't make the curve. Who is to say we weren't telling the truth?"

Kerry didn't answer him. There was no answer for this boy.

Instead of being ashamed, of admitting his wrong, he didn't feel one bit of guilt. He was, instead, planning how to circumvent the law and his parents. But then his parents were at fault, too, for letting him get off, blameless, after the previous accident.

Ten minutes later, the ambulance siren wailed faintly in the distance, and Duke was driven off to the hospital.

When Kerry got in beside Mark, she said gratefully, "It feels good to be in where it is warm."

"I never thought of that, Kerry. I am sorry," he apologized. "You probably caught cold—in that gown."

"I guess I didn't think of it myself," she admitted.

"I guess I didn't realize either what I was asking you to do, Kerry. It is just that, when I saw Duke lying there, I remembered what those kids did to my father."

"I understand, Mark. I am the one who should apologize. For being so childish."

"Not childish. Just a normal female. I told you. That is what I like about you. You make a guy feel protective and masculine."

She smiled to herself. Me and Mom and a million other women. The weaker sex. But all the while we have to be strong without your knowing it.

When they reached her house, Kerry was shaking so that she could scarcely walk. She stopped outside the door.

"I can't face them, Mark! What will I say?" she whispered.

"Do you want me to tell them? The truth? That we were parked at Poplar Pond? And that we saw the drag race?"

"I don't know!" she cried. But she knew he was right.

He peered down at her. "You *do* want me to. Come on, let's get it over."

They walked quietly down the hall to the living room, but it was empty; there was only a dim light on next to her father's chair.

"They must have gone to bed," she whispered.

"Do you want me to come over tomorrow and explain?" he asked softly.

"Maybe they went to bed early," she said hopefully. "Maybe they don't know what time I came in."

"I still think you ought to tell them. If you don't and they find out, they will never trust me again. If you don't explain, Kerry, I will."

"I will! I will! Tomorrow morning," she promised.

"And I shouldn't have come in this late, Kerry. It is almost three."

He put his arms around her, kissed her lightly and said, "Good night, Kerry. And don't worry."

He can say that, she thought as she wearily tiptoed up the stairs. He doesn't have to face my mother and father tomorrow morning!

CHAPTER XVII

But it wasn't as bad as she expected. Her mother woke her at noon. She was starved despite the fact that she was worried about her parents' reaction to her confession. She ate a huge breakfast. Nervously she made a mound of the muffin crumbs on her plate, debating the proper approach to the events of the previous night.

Her mother did it for her. "Kerry," she asked, "do you think Mark and his mother would like to come to dinner on Thanksgiving?"

"Mom," she murmured, "you might not want Mark to come here again."

They all stared at her.

"What does that mean?" her father snapped.

"You mean because you didn't get home 'til almost three?" her mother inquired. "We were awake and heard you come in."

"You brought Mark in, didn't you?" her father accused. "Don't ever do that again! At three o'clock in the morning!"

"Brad, I am sure she has an explanation," her mother said soothingly.

"Mom!" she plunged in. "Mom! We didn't come straight home last night. We—we were parked out at Poplar Pond!"

There was no visible reaction. Her mother's face was impassive; her father's, frowning. But he often looked that way when he was only thinking deeply. For a moment she thought she caught the trace of a faint smile on Grandma's face. But it couldn't be. Grandma's remarks would probably be the most caustic of all.

If they would only say something! But they didn't. All three waited, silently, for her to continue. Unnerved, she shredded a muffin into tiny piles on her plate and then raced into a recounting of the events of the previous night. She told them about Mark's reason for taking her out to the pond; she told them about the discussion of marriage. But she couldn't reveal his statements about necking. She was afraid of her father's ire and her grandma's sarcasm. Her mother would understand, she knew. And she resolved to tell her mother when they were alone.

"Mark came in with me because he didn't think that I—he thought that he ought to explain," she concluded, still staring at her plate, not daring to look up.

For a minute, the only sound in the dining room was the soft sibilance of the tea kettle, steaming on the kitchen stove.

"Good girl." Her father was the first one to speak. She looked up at him in amazement. Wasn't he going to reprimand her?

"Good boy, too," her grandmother remarked. "Knew he had a head on his shoulders."

"Don't look astonished, Kerry," her mother said. "Did you think we were going to clap you in irons? For being an hour late? It is just that we worry. But we think you and Mark did a fine thing. You could have left that boy there and no one would have been the wiser."

"I wanted to," Kerry recalled.

"But you didn't," her father said.

"If you had only called," her mother began.

"We couldn't! There wasn't any 'phone!"

"Mark could have called from the hospital," her mother protested.

"I guess he was so upset he didn't think of that," Kerry answered.

"About this parking," her father said sternly. "There is no reason why you two have to go off into the woods! You can park right here in the living room. That way you won't get into trouble."

Kerry flushed. *He makes it sound so sordid. If he only knew what Mark was like! If he only knew what Mark had said last night!*

"Did it yourself. Got a short memory, haven't you?" Her grandmother spoke suddenly.

"Who did what, Mother?" Mr. Kendall asked.

"You. You and Kit. Parked. Remember?"

Her father was speechless.

"You and Kit used to park. Remember the time near the baseball field? You got stuck in the mud, and when you tried to get out, you wound up in center field? Had to walk two miles to get home, you and Kit. And next morning, the garageman had to haul the car out. Borrowed the car, too. Remember?"

Kerry was startled. Her mother and father? Her *father?* He is so straight-laced!

"Now, Grandma," her mother laughed. "You know that when Brad and I were going together, my parents weren't living. I had an apartment."

"And you didn't expect me to visit Kit in her apartment, did you?" Her father was flustered.

"Didn't say anything about that. Just reminding you that Kerry and Mark didn't invent the pastime."

With that, all four of them burst out laughing.

And that was that. No recriminations, no threats. Kerry breathed a sigh of relief. I am glad it is over!

Except for one thing. After Mr. Kendall and Grandma had left to do some shopping in town, Mrs. Kendall told Kerry she wanted to talk to her. When they were settled on the couch, Kerry waited uncertainly.

"Kerry," she began, "it isn't that Dad and I don't trust you, both you and Mark. We do. You are almost eighteen. You are a woman, with all the emotions and desires of a woman. And you have been taught the difference between right and wrong. If you don't know it now, then Dad and I have failed as parents. But you are in love. And what seems right for the moment may be wrong, hopelessly wrong. Oh, I know that some people would scoff at two eighteen-year-old high school seniors being in love. But it has been happening for hundreds, thousands of

years. But today it is not possible, not practical to—to con-
sumate that love. You understand what I am talking about?"

Kerry nodded. This is what Mark was saying last night.
Wait until I tell her! She will be so happy! She won't have
any doubts about either one of us.

"When Grandma was young, teen-agers—I hate that word—
young people could fall in love and marry right away. But
today,—when a college education is practically a must for those
who have the ability—well, I guess even Romeo and Juliet
would get their diplomas before they eloped," she laughed.

Kerry grinned. Then, seriously, she began, "Mom, I want to
tell you what Mark said—"

"Hear me out, Kerry," her mother interrupted. "Let me finish. You and Mark are bright; you have ability. We want you
to use it. We want you to be graduated from college. So—don't
let—don't let an impulse make you lose sight of the future."

"Mom, that is what I wanted to tell you." She repeated the
discussion she and Mark had had the night before. When she
had finished, she asked, "Now do you see? He believes as you
do."

"As every parent does," her mother remarked.

"So you don't have to worry about us, Mom. Mark has a
'No Parking' sign on his car."

Her mother took Kerry's hand in hers. "You are a lucky girl.
Mark respects you. At least, I hope he is being honest with
you." She reflected a moment. "I realize he is more mature than
most boys his age, but when I think of it, it seems a little
strange that he—"

"Mom. I believe him and I believe *in* him. Oh, he does sound a little pompous sometimes. He's even arrogant. But that is the way he is. He is a writer. At least, he is going to be."

"Oh, I don't think writers are any different from anyone else. I suppose, being brought up without a father, he has *had* to mature sooner . . ."

She turned and looked searchingly at Kerry.

"Anyway, it is the girl, the woman who decides. Remember that, Kerry. If you respect yourself, a boy will respect you."

"I know, Mom."

"Now," she said, "why don't you call Mark and ask him and his mother about Thanksgiving?"

I am fortunate, Kerry realized. I can talk my problems over with Mom. Lots of girls can't. I have always been able to confide in her, from the time I was very small. Perhaps because I was a child among three adults. It made me feel important to be able to discuss things with my mother. It was the one way I could hurdle the wall, the one way I could enter their adult world.

When she called Mark and told him about her parents' calm reception of her story, he simply remarked, "I told you so." And he and his mother were delighted to accept Mrs. Kendall's invitation to dinner.

Duke appeared on Monday, flaunting the cast on his arm, and spent the day getting autographs. He didn't ask Kerry for her signature, however, nor did the other boys who had danced with her at the Frolic make any effort to be friendly. She thought it strange, and she mentioned it to Mark.

"Look, Kerry," he said, "I thought you were over that. I thought you were finally convinced that they weren't going to ask you to join their select circle."

"But why did Kenny and all the others—"

"Kenny is a peculiar guy. I think—I think—if I got to know him—I would like him. I think he is a lot like me."

"Oh, Mark! There isn't any resemblance whatsoever!"

"I don't know. I have a feeling that we might—that we could be tuned to the same wave length," he reflected.

"I don't see how."

"Well, I don't expect to be his buddy, so we will never know. Anyway, I think he wanted to thank you. Or, at least, he thought he ought to thank you for that Clarence Darrow bit in Ford's class."

I can't tell whether or not he is being sarcastic, Kerry thought. I think he is jealous.

"But he is the strong, silent type, I guess," Mark continued. "So the only way he knew how to thank you was to dance with you. When the other guys saw that, they decided to show their loyalty to him by doing the same. I think they figured he would beat Duke in the drag race. Even if he didn't, it was good insurance."

"It is not very flattering that I was used as a—as a—"

"As a sacrificial lamb, a peace offering before the great god Sanford? Look, Kerry, they probably were sincere when they told you how much they admired you for taking Kenny's part. They are not bad kids. It is just that they are the kind that need to belong. They don't have enough to make it on their own so they have to run with the pack. And they don't understand anyone who won't or doesn't want to. They flipped when I turned down their invitation," he boasted smugly.

I don't understand either, she thought. The only reason why I am content now is that I have Mark. What if, by some miracle, I should be asked to join the Crew? Would I refuse? What if it meant losing Mark? And it would. She couldn't truthfully answer the question.

Thanksgiving Day was grey and cold, a still, expectant cold. Mark insisted after dinner that he had to go out and get some air or he would fall sound asleep. He and Kerry walked up to the Sanford garage and stables and around the formal gardens, withered and bleak beneath the dreary sky.

"Does Kenny ever drive out this way?" he asked as they walked back down the driveway to Kerry's house.

"No. This is the rear entrance," she explained. "The main road is on the other side of the house."

"But doesn't he keep his car in the garage?" he persisted.

"Yes, but he goes out the front of the garage. Why would he come out this way?"

"I guess he wouldn't," Mark answered. "I was just wondering."

Kerry hid her face in her coat collar. He is jealous! The self-sufficient Mark Lee! He is afraid that now that Kenny has noticed me, he might just take it into his head to drop by. What if he did? He might. Oh, but that is just wishful thinking, she decided, dismissing the possibility from her mind.

CHAPTER XVIII

On Christmas Day, when she and Mark exchanged gifts, they first looked at the presents and then at each other. The packages were both the same size and shape. "Two minds with a single thought," Mark commented happily as he carefully removed the gold paper. He was delighted with her gift, a slim volume of Keats' poetry. He had given her Elizabeth Barrett Browning's poems.

"Tonight, after I am gone," he whispered, as they sat on the floor by the Christmas tree, "look at page 7."

She was so exhausted when she went to bed she fell sound asleep immediately and forgot what Mark had asked her to do. Somehow, she never did discover the poem he wanted her to read, not until several months later.

Exhausted by the holiday activities, the students trudged dismally back to school in January. The dreary prospect of impending mid-year exams swung over them menacingly. But, like the glimmering of light at the end of a tunnel, for seniors at any rate, was the Senior Banquet which would be held on the Friday night after exams.

Kerry bought a white silk jersey gown, white satin heels, and a delicate rhinestone tiara for the banquet. With the sizable check Grandma had given her for Christmas she bought a soft white fur jacket.

Two days before the banquet, Mark asked her if she would like to interview Merry Raleigh for the school paper. The agency for which Merry modeled was sending photographers to the banquet. A national magazine for teen-agers was planning a series on high school social affairs and the first one would feature Merry.

Kerry didn't like the assignment; she approached Merry reluctantly. The other girl, however, was very cooperative. She sat with Kerry for an hour in the auditorium, describing the disadvantages as well as the advantages of modeling. She explained that she had gotten into the field quite by accident. Her father was an advertising executive, and one of his clients, seeing her picture on Mr. Raleigh's desk, had suggested using her for a campaign. As a joke more than anything else, her father had taken her to Bjorne, the top commercial photographer in the country. She was so photogenic that Bjorne hired her himself.

"Are you planning to continue when you go to college?" Kerry asked.

"No! Definitely not!" Merry answered. "It has been too confining. Why, do you know, Kerry, I can't go skiing! I might break a leg in the middle of a campaign. I can't go swimming.

Might get tanned. I can't even eat what I like. If I put on a few pounds, the camera doubles them! No, I am *not* going to model after this year! What I really want to do is to go into fashion design."

"And then model your own creations?"

"Not on your life! I want to be on the outside looking in," she laughed.

"How do you ever resist food?" Kerry answered, closing her notebook. "I couldn't."

"It was hard in the beginning," Merry admitted. "Now I just nibble on fruit when I am hungry. Or carrots! I have eaten tons of carrots! It's a wonder I don't turn into a rabbit," she said, twitching her nose.

When Kerry told Mark later that she had been surprised at the other girl's friendliness, he said, "I told you that those kids aren't ogres. It is just status, that's all. They will all go to Ivy League colleges, join the 'right' sorority or fraternity, get a job with the 'right' company when they graduate, live in the 'right' part of town, join the 'right' country club. Read Vance Packard. He has said it all. Well, I hope not *all*. I want to—I intend to say it—to write it—some day."

Jamie and Andrea had double-dated with Kerry and Mark on the week-ends when Jamie had been able to come up from the city, and Andrea suggested that they go to the banquet together. She announced with glee that her father was going to let them take his Cadillac.

"He likes Jamie so much," she said when she called to tell Kerry what time they would pick her up, "he would give him anything! Probably because he thought he would never marry me off. Now he sees a potential victim for me to drag down the aisle," she jeered.

"You idiot!" Kerry laughed. "You know Jamie would elope with you if you asked him to."

"Hey, chum! Let's. All four of us!"

"Not me."

"Oh, I forgot. Mr. Mark Lee and his four-year plan," she giggled.

Kerry had told her how Mark felt about marriage. The other had been strangely silent, had made no comment, until now.

"I agree with him," retorted Kerry hotly. "So does my mother. It is foolish for two people who are going to college to even think of getting married before they graduate. And maybe get tied down with a family—"

"Take it easy, chum! I was just kidding," Andrea interrupted. "You are entitled to your opinion and I am entitled to mine."

But she doesn't express her opinion. She isn't thinking of marriage, is she, Kerry wondered. Jamie has years ahead of him before he finishes his studies!

"What is your opinion, Andrea?" she asked hesitantly.

"That is a long story, and, if I started to tell you, we would never make the banquet. Sybil is signaling me now. It is time to start getting ready."

She has become almost secretive since she has been going steady, Kerry realized. But then, she admitted guiltily, so have I. I don't tell her everything about Mark and me.

"Mom has been calling me, too, for the past five minutes. See you at nine, Andrea."

"Wait a minute. Sybil wants me to ask you something. She

wants to know if your mother would let you go with Amos and her and Jamie and me—and you and Mark—over the Washington's Birthday Holiday. We get four days off from school."

"Go where?"

"Up to Telemark Ridge. It is a ski resort in Vermont."

"I would love it, Andrea! I am not the world's best skier, though. Dad did teach me when we lived out in the country, but I don't know how good I am."

"Listen, chum. You are talking to the original snow bunny." Andrea giggled. "But that doesn't make any difference. It will be fun."

"All right. I'll ask Mom. I know she'll let me."

"Kerry! Will you get off that 'phone and start getting ready?" her mother called.

"I heard her," laughed Andrea. "See you."

"You look like a snow queen," whispered Mark as they settled in the back of the car on the way to the banquet that night. "You glitter and sparkle tonight."

When she walked across the dance floor of the Cabin to their table, she was aware of heads turning. Even Kenny stared at her, and, somehow, she thought there was frank admiration in his eyes, instead of the usual impassive arrogance.

Merry, however, was the center of attraction. The photographers shot her from all angles. She was in red, bright red velvet that traced her slimness and highlighted the ink-black of her hair. It was obvious that she was a professional; she walked, she sat, she laughed as though she were an automaton.

As Kerry and Mark got up to dance, a flash bulb blinded them. The photographer, who was squatting on the floor and angling his camera up at them, asked, "Mind if I follow you around the floor?" Puzzled, Kerry and Mark simply smiled and shrugged. After he had taken a dozen shots, he thanked them and joined the other men at a table. Kerry watched him curiously. He kept pointing to her and Mark; he seemed to be trying to explain something.

"What's with that character?" Jamie asked as they sat down at the table.

"Oh, I always knew that craggy face of Mark's would be glowering from the movie screen some day," joked Andrea.

"It wasn't I. It was Kerry they were interested in," said Mark.

"Maybe you will be giving Miss Raleigh some competition?" Andrea giggled.

"Oh, Andrea! She is a professional model!" Even though she was flattered, Kerry was embarrassed.

"What magazine are the pictures of Merry going to be in?" asked Jamie. "I'd like to see them. Maybe we will all be in it."

"It's called *The Teen-Ager*," Kerry explained.

"Now that's an original title," commented Mark.

Just then the senior class president tapped his spoon against his glass and called them to order. Speeches and awards followed. Mark was genuinely surprised when he was selected as "the most creative." Neither Andrea nor Kerry was mentioned; they hadn't expected to be singled out. But Kerry felt a little stab of jealousy when Merry was chosen as "the most attractive." Kenny Sanford's face relaxed slightly when he was named "best-looking boy."

After the affair, as the foursome was leaving, the photographer asked Kerry to pose in the doorway.

"Say, maybe you will be in *The Teen-Ager*," Andrea said seriously.

"Let's forget it, Andrea," Mark snapped. "He probably just wanted some shots of an attractive girl."

"Attractive? She's positively beautiful tonight! Or hadn't you noticed?" Andrea teased.

"Let's forget it," Kerry said. "I am interested in more important things—like food. Mom is going to fix breakfast for us."

"Breakfast?" Jamie asked. "It's only three o'clock!"

"I thought we could go home, dance, or just sit around for awhile and then have breakfast," Kerry explained.

"It's a good idea. Some of the kids are going into the city, but I think the driving on these icy roads would be rough, don't you, Jamie?" Mark asked soberly.

"I certainly wouldn't take Dr. Stark's car," Jamie agreed.

When they arrived at Kerry's house, they were tired and sleepy. No one wanted to dance. Andrea kicked off her shoes, tucked her feet under her and sat on the couch in the circle of Jamie's arm. Kerry and Mark sat at the opposite end. Drowsily, they talked for an hour. Then Kerry went upstairs, changed into a sweater and slacks and prepared breakfast.

Just before dawn the other three left and Kerry staggered wearily off to bed. For the first time in many months she dreamed; she dreamed that she was strolling nonchalantly down the platform at Atlantic City during the Miss America pageant, while people on all sides were applauding wildly for her. Flash bulbs exploded in rapid succession as she smiled at the audience; soon they became so bright she had to squint to see where she was going.

"Kerry? Kerry? It's two o'clock. Do you want to get up?"

Her mother had raised the shade and a brilliant winter sun flooded the room.

"I was just—I just had a dream," she stammered, sitting up slowly and groggily.

But she never told anyone about the dream. Not anyone, not even Mark. And she forgot the photographers at the banquet. Or she thought she had.

CHAPTER XIX

When Merry Raleigh called her a week later, Kerry realized, deep down, that she was still thinking of the banquet, still wondering why she and Mark had been photographed so many times.

"Kerry?" The other girl sounded cool, aloof. "This is Merry Raleigh."

"Hi," Kerry answered. What is she calling me for? Maybe to thank me for the article I wrote about her for the school paper. Everyone said it was very good. Or is it to tell me something about—about my pictures? That they are going to be in *The Teen-Ager?* That would make the kids sit up and take notice! Especially the Crew!

"Kerry, Mr. Milliken, the one who did the shots for the magazine at the banquet? Remember?"

"Yes." It *was* about the pictures! Her heart thudded so loud she was sure that Merry could hear it! The hand holding the telephone trembled, and she had to grasp it with both hands.

"Well, he was impressed with the shots he took of you. He says you are photogenic, and he wants to know whether or not you would be interested in doing some modeling."

Kerry couldn't answer. Her mouth was dry; her vocal chords paralyzed. Her hands were welded to the telephone.

"Kerry? Did you hear me?"

"I heard you," she croaked hoarsely.

"What is the matter? You don't sound very enthusiastic."

"It—it isn't that. It is just that—it is just that it is such a—such a surprise," she managed to stammer. "I don't know what to say! I have never done anything like that! I wouldn't know what to do—"

Merry laughed. "If you are interested, I will show you the ropes. There is more to it than meets the eye. And that is no pun!"

"I know, Merry. You told me during the interview."

"Not all, Kerry. Not all. But why don't you think about it and let me know. You don't have to decide this very minute."

"All right, I will." If she only knew! I *want* to say yes, but I can't! "Thanks, Merry, for calling."

"You may not thank me if you really get involved in this rat race. Call me, Kerry."

Kerry had difficulty in replacing the telephone. Her fingers were stiff; her hands, immobile. Her legs felt detached from her body, as though they were moving involuntarily. Robot-like, she walked slowly down the hall.

"Mom," she announced shakily, "they want me to model."
Her mother's face swam before her, dim and hazy.

"Kerry! What is the matter? You look ill! Sit down!" Her
mother's voice came from a'distance.

"Didn't you hear me, Mom? Merry Raleigh just called and
they want me to model!"

"Well, if it affects you this way, I don't think it is such a
good idea," her mother remarked, feeling Kerry's forehead. "I
thought you weren't feeling good. Sit down and relax."

Her mother was acting strangely. She didn't seem impressed.

"Mom!" she persisted as she slumped into a chair, "didn't
you *hear* me?"

"Of course I did. But don't look so frightened. I was in a
fashion show myself when I was in high school. It isn't too
difficult. Oh, you do get jittery just before you go out on the
stage but—"

Kerry began to laugh uncontrollably.

"Now what is funny? I admit I am no prize beauty," her
mother protested, "but I did manage to sashay rather calmly
across the stage. Kerry! What *is* the matter?"

Kerry was hysterical. She alternately wept and giggled. The
shock of Merry's news and the somnambulism into which it
had plunged her were dispelled now by her mother's matter-
of-fact assumption that she was to model clothes in a local
fashion show.

"Oh, Mom! You are precious!" she managed to gulp. "You
think—you think—I mean—" She couldn't finish. She shrieked
with laughter.

"Kerry! Stop it!" Her mother was worried.

Still giggling sporadically, Kerry wiped her eyes and looked happily up at her mother. She is like a halter for Dad and me. She keeps us from swerving off the track. It is because she is so sensible in her quiet way. I wish I could be like her. I am so mixed up at times. I really don't know what I want.

"Well, that is much better," her mother said, patting her on the head. "Now maybe you will tell me what sparked this paroxysm?"

"It isn't what you think, Mom. Remember my telling you about what happened at Senior Banquet? About Merry's posing for the magazine? And about the pictures they took of Mark and me? Well, the man who took the pictures wants me to model!"

"You mean professionally?"

"I guess so. Merry told me to think it over, decide, and call her back."

"But you haven't finished high school! How could you?"

"Merry does it afternoons. She has her school schedule arranged so that she can go into the city right after lunch. And sometimes she has Saturday assignments. Mom! Think of the money I could make! And save for college!"

Her mother picked up the corner of her apron and slowly rubbed the top of the table. She looks so much better, Kerry realized; she has even put on some weight. Her face isn't drawn and taut any more. When she smiles, her cheeks dimple.

"Kerry, why don't we wait until your father gets home and see what he says," her mother suggested.

"Oh, Mom! He will probably say that I can't! You know him! Besides, why do we have to ask him. You are the boss," she said boldly.

"Don't ever let me hear you say that again! Your father is

the—boss—as you call him! If he disapproves, you will *not* do it!"

To Kerry's surprise, her father was agreeable. He did stipulate however that if her marks at school should suffer, she was to promise to give up modeling. She agreed fervently.

When she called Merry, the other girl told her that Mr. Milliken was planning another series for the magazine. This one was to feature girls' athletics in high school, and he wanted to star Kerry. He also planned to begin immediately.

Andrea squealed with delight at the news but Mark merely commented that she would get tired of the whole thing before long.

The next week was a hectic one. Every day after school, Kerry was whisked from one place to another, from the gymnasium to the pool, from the basketball court to a snow-covered slope outside of town where she stood poised, for a long, long hour, in a furred parka, ski pants and boots, at the top of the hill while Mr. Milliken plowed up and down through the knee-deep snow, snapping her from all sides.

When she got home, she was sniffling, and, by the time she was ready for bed, she had a sore throat. Her mother informed her emphatically that this was the end. No daughter of hers was going to jeopardize her health for a few pictures. Fully aware that her mother meant what she said, Kerry docilely gargled, sprayed her throat, swallowed medication. By morning, she felt better, and, by afternoon, any trace of a cold had disappeared.

She called her mother after dismissal, told her that she had recovered, and insisted that she *had* to complete the assignment. It was to be indoor shots of girls' track activities to be taken inside on the practice track which circled above the gymnasium balcony. Reluctantly her mother agreed, warning her that there would be no more modeling if it were to result in illness.

At five o'clock Mr. Milliken gathered his paraphernalia and told her he was "wrapping up" the job. He walked wearily across the floor, turned momentarily, and thanked her. Grudgingly he told her that she was a "natural," that she could, she should continue with modeling. Then, almost as though he were sorry for his compliments, he squashed his hat down over his ears and trudged out.

That night, thoroughly exhausted, she just about managed to drag herself to the dinner table. For the first time in her life, food held no appeal for her. She just wanted to lie down and sleep, sleep for a week.

"What is the matter?" her mother asked. "You are not getting another sore throat?"

"No, Mom. I am just tired."

"So you have found out that it isn't so glamorous after all?" her father commented. "It is a good thing that it is all over."

"This assignment, Dad, but there will be others."

"I don't think so," her father declared. "Your mother and I agreed to this one just so that you could have a taste of it. But we have no intention of permitting you to continue."

"But, Dad! You didn't say that in the beginning!"

"Look at yourself!" he answered angrily. "You have deep circles under your eyes; you look as though you are ready to collapse any minute. You *can't* hold down two jobs! School is your job right now, the important one."

"It is just that it is all so new! I will get used to it!" Kerry protested.

"No!" There was finality, unquestioned finality, in his tone.

"Couldn't I just have some studio portraits made?" she wheedled.

"What are they?" her father asked.

"Well, Merry says that you have some taken and then you go around to agencies with them. And you get assignments—"

"Didn't I tell you that you are finished?" her father snapped.

"Let the child do it," Grandma said suddenly. "Can't hurt her."

Speechless, Mr. Kendall stared at his mother.

"Brad," her mother suggested, "why can't she? Of course, she is exhausted, but it is only the first time."

"You were the one who said that the novelty would wear off and she would be contented with this one—assignment, or whatever they call it," he answered.

"I know. And I think Kerry realizes that this isn't her life's work that she is getting involved in. It will be just for the rest of the school year. And maybe for the summer."

"For the summer? Haven't you told her?"

"Told me what?" Kerry looked questioningly at her mother and then at her father.

"Nothing," Mrs. Kendall said abruptly. "You find out from Merry about the arrangements for the portraits and we will go into the city some Saturday."

"Kit, I don't think you ought to be traveling into the city," her father said.

"Nonsense!" Grandma sniffed. "Leave her alone."

Kerry gaped at all three of them. What was going on? Were they going to shut her out again? Was her mother ill? But she couldn't be! Not Mom. It was true that Grandma wasn't looking too well. She had lost weight; she tired easily. She sat alone in her room a great deal, her knitting neglected on her lap, just gazing out at the trees and the sky. That must be it, Kerry decided. Maybe Mom and Dad are worried about her, and Dad doesn't want Mom going into the city, just in case Grandma might be taken ill suddenly. But what about next summer? Perhaps Mom will have to be in constant attendance upon Grandma if she has to be confined to her bed. And I will have to take care of the house! It isn't fair, she fretted.

"Don't look so woebegone," her mother said. "Call Merry."

Merry informed her that Bjorne was the man to go to; he was tops in the photography field. She indicated that he would be frank with Kerry; he would tell her whether or not he thought she should invest in portraits. They were expensive, she added. When she mentioned the actual cost, Kerry was startled. Her parents would never give her that much money!

Then she realized that she could use part of the fee that she had coming from the *Teen-Ager* assignment to pay Bjorne. Her father was shocked when she told him how much the portraits would cost.

"I am going to use money I made from the magazine job. It is my money," she reminded him.

"I thought you were going to save that for college," he said.

"I can make *more* this way," she insisted.

"Don't have to worry about college," Grandma said. "She will have enough for that. I will see to it."

Kerry smiled gratefully at her. Feeling guilty and ashamed, she remembered that she had dreaded the household chores that would be her responsibility if her grandmother should have another heart attack.

So it was settled. Before they could change their minds,

Kerry called Bjorne for an appointment. His secretary asked her to come to the studio on the day after Washington's Birthday.

Saturday was a let-down. She wandered around the house all afternoon. She hadn't seen Mark for an entire week, except between classes. She hadn't been able to meet him after school because of her work with Mr. Milliken. Her mother had driven in to pick her up; she had said that she didn't think it was fair for Kerry to expect him to wait around. And he hadn't called her.

Restless, unable to concentrate on anything, she decided to go for a walk before dinner. As she opened the gate, Mark drove up.

"Going somewhere?" he asked as he got out of the car.

"Just for a walk. I got bored sitting around," she confessed.

"You mean the bloom is off the rose? Now that you have had your fling?" he jeered.

He is jealous, Kerry realized. He doesn't want me to think of anything except him. And I thought he would be proud of me!

"I am only beginning," she boasted. She told him about her plans.

"Kerry, I think you are foolish. What do you expect to get out of this? You certainly aren't going to make a career out of it. You won't have time for anything else. Your senior year in high school! You already missed a whole week of assignments for the paper, you know."

"I don't expect to get anything out of it except satisfaction."

"What does that mean?" He took her arm, swung her around, and peered at her in the dusk.

"I'm not sure," she admitted. "Maybe I have felt left out of things—always—since I was small. Maybe I am insecure; I lack confidence. And this modeling will give it to me. Or maybe I just like being the center of attention."

"Who says you are the center of attention? You mean, just because of that one spread in that stupid magazine? It hasn't even come out yet. And your face may be left on the cutting room floor," he sneered. "Even if this Bjorne does do the pictures, that's no guarantee that you will make the big time."

"Well, whether I do or not, will be no concern of yours from now on. That's for sure! I thought you would be proud of me, that you would get as much of a kick out of it as I do. What's the matter? Jealous?" she jeered.

"Don't be childish, Kerry. I thought you were beginning to grow up, but you're not. Go ahead. Have fun with your new plaything. As you say, it will be no concern of mine." He wheeled into the darkness. As he reached the car, he turned and said, "It might interest you to know that your appointment is right in the middle of the week-end we were supposed to go to Telemark. I am going anyway!" He slammed the door and spun down the drive, geysers of snow cascading in his wake.

She walked slowly back to the house, angrily kicking the snow that was piled on the side of the driveway. I will call Andrea and explain why I can't go skiing with them. She will understand even if Mark doesn't. He *is* jealous! He wants me to himself. Does he expect me to follow him around meekly for the next four years? I can be a person in my own right now. I can be important. He doesn't want that. Well, I *do!* I want it and I am going to have it, she vowed.

But that night she lay awake, unable to sleep. Over the

images of herself on magazine covers was super-imposed Mark's face, the strong, firm mouth, the dark, brooding eyes. And, as though he were in the room with her, she could hear his voice, the deep voice that thrilled her even now, after all these months. She couldn't recall the angry words that had passed between them a few hours before. She could only remember, with exquisite pain, his ardor when he whispered gently, "I love you, Kerry."

She cried herself to sleep that night.

CHAPTER XX

Andrea did understand. At least, she seemed to. She doesn't seem too disappointed that I am not going, Kerry realized ruefully. She is so much in love with Jamie that she isn't aware of much of anything else. I thought that I was in love, too. If I were, if I really were, I would be willing to give up this new career. But I couldn't be happy that way. I don't want to be Mark's shadow; I want to be *somebody* on my own. Modeling will give me importance. And yet, despite her apparent conviction, she felt a tiny doubt dragging, dragging down deep.

She and her mother left for the city early on the day of the appointment. Bjorne's studio was on a side street near the East River. When they got out of the taxi, Kerry shivered in the damp bitterness of the gusts off the river. The wind flicked pieces of dirty paper from the gutter and plastered them against the shabby brownstone buildings. Pedestrians, their faces impersonal masks, scurried by, oblivious. Kerry walked close to her mother. She didn't like this drab, bedraggled city.

The one-story studio was sandwiched between two, tall seedy buildings. Its façade was white brick; beneath its single window was a bright-red window box, containing sere brown stalks that rustled in the wind. Kerry and her mother waited in the tiny office while the secretary announced their arrival. Kerry was disappointed. She didn't know what she had expected, but it certainly wasn't this miniscule room with its single desk and chair and the faded maple setee cringing in the corner.

When the secretary ushered them into the studio, Kerry gasped. It looked like a garage. It obviously had *been* a garage. Dingy white walls were covered with photographs of handsome men, charming women, lovely girls, and beautiful children. She recognized some of them. They were, or had been, the illustrations for nationally and internationally famous products. The grey concrete floor was littered with chairs, tables, rolled-up rugs, discarded costumes, artificial flowers, children's toys. At one end it was bare except for a stool which stood in front of what looked like a white shade attached to the wall.

Bjorne himself was slim and small. His black turtle-neck sweater and black chinos accentuated his suppleness and grace as he walked across the studio to greet Kerry and her mother. Kerry was startled to see that he was wearing black thong sandals. She wondered how he could stand it; the room was icy cold.

He directed her to a dressing room, informing her that she was to wear a sweater and skirt. When she protested that she had brought an evening gown, he waved his hands back and forth before his face and closed his eyes as though in pain.

"You are a girl. Yes? Not a woman. You wear, therefore, a sweater and skirt. If you want to play actress, you go to Coney Island and have the portrait taken there? Yes?"

"I—I am wearing a sweater and skirt," she said. She was a little bit afraid of this temperamental man.

"Let us see," he suggested.

She took her coat off and stood stiffly at attention.

"Good! That is good! Just right! Come. Over here and sit on the stool."

Mrs. Kendall settled back on a huge brown velvet couch that sagged in the middle. She smiled reassuringly at her daughter and picked up a magazine from the ornate table in front of her. Kerry grinned. She is trying to give me confidence. She knows I am a little frightened. She wants me to relax.

"That is it! Unwind, child," Bjorne advised. "You are a little uneasy? That is natural. People do that. They pose. You do not pose when the picture is taken. You just sit and think. Happy, maybe sad thoughts. But never think 'I am having my picture taken!' Never!"

She followed his advice. All the while he was working, she thought of the pool, of swimming in its cool, clear water; of the Football Frolic; of Kenneth Sanford; of the lush beauty of the roses in the greenhouse; of Andrea and her brother. And then she thought of Mark. Like a film strip, his face unreeled before her. She couldn't erase his image.

"That is enough," Bjorne said soothingly. "That thought you must replace. That is enough sadness."

At his words, the film broke and Mark disappeared, to be

replaced by images of her bedroom, of Grandma, of the old house. Bjorne turned her face, tipped her head, curved her back. Each time it was only a slight change from the previous pose, but it made her feel different. The hot, white lights seeped into her skin—into her brain.

After an hour, he stood back from his camera and announced, "It is done. Thank you to the patient mother." He nodded in Mrs. Kendall's direction. "And you, child. Thank you. It has been a joy this afternoon." He accompanied them both to the door of the studio.

Is this all, wondered Kerry. This gaunt, desolate room? These time-worn props? Those lonely floodlights? She had pictured herself, glittering and sophisticated, against silver draperies; chic and poised, against a plush background.

"You want to know what I think? Yes? Whether you should try to be up there with them?" He pointed at the collage of beauty on the walls. "You have the face and, what is of more importance, you have the feelings. Your face is like the sunlight and clouds, mirrored in the water. You are very pliable. Yes, you could do it."

Kerry held her breath. She squeezed her mother's hand. She could scarcely contain herself. She wanted to hurry outside and hug and kiss her mother. She was going to be a model! Bjorne, the famous Bjorne, had said so!

"But should you? I do not know. If this is the only thing you want to do, if it is a craving inside you, then try it. But if not? I think no. It is not worth it unless you must do it. You must lose the weight. Fifteen pounds, I think."

"Fifteen pounds!" Kerry cried.

"At least. And the hair. It must be cut. It gives a maturity now. It does not fit the face, the rare childlike face that you have. It is that you are on the border, between the child and the woman. That is what the camera sees. That is what you can sell. If you have to." He sighed. "Good afternoon, mother. Good afternoon, child." Mrs. Kendall murmured, "Thank you," as he closed the door after them.

After the secretary had noted their name and address, they left. Neither of them said a word until they reached the parking lot uptown where they had left the car.

"Mom! You didn't say a word all afternoon!" Kerry accused.

"What did you want me to say?" her mother asked gently.

"Well, what do you think? He did say I had a chance, didn't he?" she asked.

"Yes."

"So? Do you think I ought to—to do all those things? Go on a diet? Cut my hair?"

"That is up to you, Kerry," her mother answered quietly. "To be perfectly frank, your father and I hadn't really planned to let you go this far. The magazine assignment, that was fine. But this professional modeling. I don't know. I talked to Mrs. Raleigh and she says it is difficult. If you lived in the city, or you were planning to attend college in New York, that would be a different matter. But I don't see how you are going to manage," she said soberly, as she inched out into the heavy traffic.

"Just let me try, Mother! Please! Look, maybe if I am successful, I won't go to college right away—"

"No! That we would not agree to! Your father and I want

you to have a college education. This modeling will have to be a side line."

"All right, but just let me try it for a few months."

Silently, she promised herself that she would do as she pleased once she was eighteen.

When the portraits arrived the next week, everybody agreed that she was indeed photogenic. At Merry's suggestion, she went into the city and made the rounds of the agencies, leaving pictures at each of them. She felt gauche and inexperienced when she saw the other girls who thronged the waiting rooms. They were svelte and poised; their beauty was a shining almost brittle perfection.

Although she didn't dare, quite yet, broach the question of having her hair cut, she went on a rigid diet. Andrea teased her every noon. While the latter lunched on hamburgers, potato chips, and chocolate ice cream, Kerry ate yogurt and drank skim milk. Since she and Mark were not speaking, she didn't stop at the Hut after school and this eliminated her daily Coke and English muffin. She even waved away her mother's pineapple cocoanut cake. At the end of the month she had lost ten pounds, and, although she would not admit it to anyone, she felt exhausted most of the time. Despite her fatigue, however, she exercised faithfully for an hour each night before she retired.

What was worse, however, she was nervous and irritable all the time. She snapped back rudely at Dr. Sherry one day and he asked her to stop in after school. He knew about her modeling; the whole school did. He told her he thought that she was foolish to consider discarding her plans for college. He took a college catalog out of his desk; it was a brochure from his own alma mater. When he told her that she would be able to secure a scholarship from his university, she didn't answer him. She was so tired that she could scarcely sit upright. Suddenly she realized that she had missed the school bus and that she would have to call her mother to come in to pick her up. Dr. Sherry insisted that he would drive her home, explaining that he had always wanted to meet her parents.

When they reached home, Kerry introduced the teacher, excused herself, and trudged upstairs to lie down before dinner. When her mother woke her an hour later, Dr. Sherry had left. She only picked at her food; she was so hungry that she was sick at her stomach; the smell and sight of food nauseated her.

Suddenly her father's fork clattered to his plate. "I have had enough of this!" he exploded. "Eat your dinner, Kerry!"

"I—I can't!" she stammered.

"You can and you will," he insisted. "You will stop this nonsense, right now! You will forget those pictures and that modeling and everything that goes with it!"

Completely unnerved, she burst into tears. Her mother got up and put her arms around her.

"Kerry," she said softly, "I think it is too much for you. This dieting, this running into New York on Saturday, the constant worrying about whether or not you're going to get an assignment. I think you ought to forget it for awhile."

"Mother," she sobbed. "I can't!" She couldn't tell her that she had to continue because, for the first time in her life, she was *somebody*. She was on the inside looking out; she was different. Why she might even join the Crew! They might ask her, once she became famous. *The Teen-Ager* in which she had been featured would be out shortly, and then who knows what might happen.

"You have no choice," her father said angrily. "I am telling you now—"

"Brad," her mother interrupted quietly, as she sat down, "give her a little while longer. Remember my dancing?"

Kerry stared at her mother. Her dancing? What did she mean by that?

"Don't look so startled, Kerry," her mother laughed. "I never told you but I had a chance to join a ballet company when I was in college. I almost did, too. Oh, you aren't the only girl that ever wanted to be in the spotlight. Every female does, I guess. And I was annoyed with Dad, because he wouldn't—he wasn't going to college. So I thought—I will show him! I even filled one engagement with the troupe."

Kerry could scarcely believe her ears. Her mother on the stage! A ballet dancer! But that accounted for her lithe figure, her ramrod posture, her quick movements.

"But I woke up, fortunately, before it was too late. I realized that it wasn't what I really wanted. It wasn't worth the rigid physical discipline, the endless hours of practice. So I went back to my books and my Dewey Decimal System," she laughed. "And to your father."

Mr. Kendall reached across the table and took his wife's hand in his. They look as though they had just fallen in love with each other, Kerry marveled. She had noticed how tender and gentle her father had been toward her mother recently. She had attributed it to his contentment with his job, with the new house, and, perhaps, to his gratitude toward her mother for her acceptance of and her loving care of Grandma. But this was different, somehow. She had heard of second childhood but never of second love, not for middle-aged husbands and wives.

"So I thought you ought to have your chance to strut your hour upon the stage," her mother continued. "And I think that you will go back to your botany. Dr. Sherry, does, too. He told us about the scholarship, about his college. It's a small one, but he told us about some of the people who have been graduated from there. Some of them are world-famous botanists."

"I know all that, Mom," Kerry agreed. "And, if you'll let me, if you'll just wait, I promise that I *will* apply to college." Let them think that anyway.

"When? In September?" Mr. Kendall asked.

"Dr. Sherry says that she has until the middle of May," her mother explained.

By that time, Kerry thought smugly, I will be all set. I will have had enough assignments to convince them that I should make modeling my career.

But there weren't any assignments; at least, she couldn't take the ones that were offered. It would have been necessary for her to take time off from school since the jobs were either for mid-morning or early afternoon. Although she pleaded with her mother, Mrs. Kendall refused to permit her to absent herself from her studies. Slowly she began to doubt that she wanted to continue. Was it worth the physical discomfort? The starvation? The eternal weariness? The dull days?

Because they *were* dull. Mark never called her any more; he never asked her for another date. At the Runes Club meetings, he treated her civilly, but he never spoke to her other than to discuss her writing for the newspaper. And Andrea was so devoted to Jamie that she had time for little else. He came up week-ends or Andrea went into the city to plays or concerts. She stayed at Jamie's house and never got back until Sunday night. They had invited Kerry to accompany them several times, but she had refused. To be without a date was bad enough; to tag along with them would have been more painful.

And then it happened! She had a call from *The Teen-Ager!* They wanted to use her for their annual Teen Queen cover! And it wouldn't be necessary for her to take time off from school; they were going to complete the shooting during Easter holidays. Her mother was unable to drive her in to the city. Grandma was really ill now; she was confined to her bed. Mrs. Kendall spent most of the day in her mother-in-law's room, reading to her or chatting with her. But Kerry didn't mind taking the train. She was so excited that she could have walked into New York!

Her mother warned her that she would be tired, that she was forfeiting the opportunity for a long rest during the vacation. At the end of the week, however, if she was tired, she was hardly aware of it. Her dreams had come true! Her face would smile up from newstands all over the country! Everyone would say, "There goes Kerry Kendall, the model!" She would be famous! No more knocking on doors. No more wanting "in."

It wasn't until she returned to school, to the daily routine, that she realized how fatigued she was. She even skipped her exercising at night. She resented the additional chores that she had to assume at home because of her grandmother's illness. A few times she neglected to clean the stove and the work counters in the kitchen. When her father discovered Mrs. Kendall doing them later in the evening, he reprimanded Kerry severely. Her only answer was a sullen silence.

But the adulation she received in school more than made up for the unpleasant aspect of life. It was easy now. She was a celebrity. She was no longer one of the anonymous crowd. Every student in school, from the meekest freshman to the most arrogant senior, knew who she was. At the center of her being was a hard core of confidence. She sauntered down the corridors, smiling mysteriously, as though she were hoarding some great secret. Occasionally she would deign to smile at someone, to flick her fingers with a bored "Hi" at the students who spoke to her. That was the way to do it. Play it cool. She hugged the new-found confidence, the armor of superiority, to her closely. She remembered the first days when, as a transfer, she had drifted aimlessly among the students, all of whom, it seemed, had been headed, like arrows, for some distant target, some important rendezvous. Now they were envious of her.

Even Mark relented enough to say, "Congratulations!" But then he added, "I hope you and your magazine cover will be very happy together." She had simply nodded graciously, smiled sweetly, and strolled away. She had to admit that he still affected her; she still thought about him often. But he had to come to her. He would have to make the first attempt at a reconciliation. And, finally, she caught the brass ring! She was invited to a party at Merry Raleigh's house! And Kenny Sanford was to be her date. Somehow she wasn't surprised. She had dreamed of acceptance by the Crew so often that she could be perfectly calm.

Although her mother didn't make any comment, Kerry knew that she did not approve. When Kenny came to pick her up, he drove down from his house. He didn't come to the door; he simply blew the horn. Her mother remonstrated, insisting that he should come in, but, before Mrs. Kendall could finish, Kerry flew out the door.

Kenny pushed the car door open and said, softly, "Hello, Kerry Kendall. Get in."

"Hi, Kenneth Sanford," she answered cooly, as she slid in beside him. If it were Mark, she thought, he would have gotten out and he would have opened the door for me. But then Mark would never have summoned her with a horn.

CHAPTER XXI

Kenny didn't say another word until they reached Merry's house. His eyes never left the road; he seemed to be an integral part of the machine. She had heard about his car. It was an Italian sports model, fast and expensive. It had been a Christmas gift from his parents.

He whipped into the Raleigh driveway and skidded to a stop. "Wait," he said, indicating that she was to get out. She stood uncertainly on the walk while he parked the car. When he returned, he started toward the door, and she followed him. He started to ring the bell, paused, and looked her full in the face. "Are you sure you want to go in?" he asked suddenly.

She stared at him. What on earth did he mean? Why had he brought her this far to ask her that?

"I don't—I don't—know what you mean," she stammered.

"No, I guess you don't," he answered curtly. "Come on."

Her confusion disappeared when they entered the living room crowded with members of the Crew. They welcomed her warmly, some of them teased her, asking when she expected to make the cover of *Life*. Mark was right, she thought happily. They *aren't* any different from the rest of the kids in school; they are just more mature, more sure of themselves.

Only Tracey Shaffer kept her distance. Kerry thought she heard the other girl mention Mark's name, but she wasn't sure. That bothers her, Kerry realized. It annoys her that he dated me. She thought that he would go back to her eventually and even agree to join the Crew if she asked him to.

But she forgot Tracey and Mark almost immediately. She danced, she talked, she laughed at the jokes. Some of the stories were obscene and not even funny, but she pretended that they were hilarious. After all, she told herself, I don't want them to think I am a prude. But she was uncomfortable. She couldn't control her blushing, and some of the boys jeered at her.

One of them insisted that she have a can of beer. To her surprise, Kenny, who had been conversing with Tiger and Neil, stood up and warned, "Lay off, you guys!" He came over to her, grasped her firmly by the arm, and steered her to a corner. "Wait here," he ordered. When he returned, he had a can of beer in one hand and a Coke in the other. He handed her the bottle and sat down on the floor at her feet. As he tilted the can, he looked up at her.

It is the first time I have ever seen him with his eyes wide open, she thought. Usually his eyes are narrowed, hooded by the lids; they have an almost furtive expression. But now, dilated, they seemed to be pleading with her.

"I didn't want to bring you here tonight," he began.

Startled, she stiffened with anger. "Then why did you? I don't have to stay. Take me home." I want to go home, she decided. I don't belong here. I was fooling myself at the beginning; I wasn't really enjoying myself. I am a little frightened; this isn't what I expected. She started to get up, but Kenny stopped her.

"No. Wait. Let me explain," he said, taking her hand.

Strange, Kerry thought, the electricity I felt the night of the Frolic isn't there. It is just a boy's hand touching mine.

"I didn't mean that I didn't want to—I don't mean that I—it isn't that—" he began.

At that moment every light in the room went out.

"What happened?" Kerry gasped.

"You see. That is what I have been trying to say. That you don't belong here. Obviously you have never been to a Crew party before. The dancing and the beer and the rest of it is just a preliminary to 'making out.' "

"But don't Merry's parents—I mean, do they approve?" she whispered in the blackness.

"None of the parents approve," he answered. "But they can't do much about it. If they protested, we would just boycott their house. And that would be social suicide for their kids," he concluded.

I could never have the Crew to my house, Kerry realized. She could visualize her father's face if he should find a darkened roomful of her friends. I don't think I would want them, she decided. I don't want them! I really don't. I don't need them.

The room was silent, except for whispers or an occasional

giggle. Frightened, Kerry sat rigidly on the edge of the chair. What a fool I was, she thought bitterly. I am not so naïve as Kenny thinks. In my sub-conscious, I *knew* that this would be the climax of the evening; I heard Mark and Andrea talking about these sessions. But I thought I could be different because I wanted so desperately to be a part of this crowd.

"Kenny, I think you had better take me home," she urged frantically.

"Let me talk to you first, Kerry," he begged softly. "It will be easier in the dark."

"And it will be easier if we leave in the dark," she suggested. "We could just slip out without their knowing it."

"We will," he promised, "but first I want to talk to you. I want to explain a few things. I don't do this often. The last time it was in Italy, when I met a girl from the States . . ." His voice drifted into the darkness.

Kerry relaxed slightly. She knew she had nothing to fear from Kenny. Or from herself. She knew now that she would not be willing to pay the price for conformity; she knew now that she didn't want "in;" she knew that the Crew, only because it was inaccessible, had been desirable. She could understand Mark's rejection of them. Mark! If he were only here! She wanted to tell him, to assure him, that she was cured. She was aware that he might not be interested, that he might not forgive her. But she could take that, too. She could wait. Some day he might come back to her.

"Kerry," Kenny began again, "I am not 'chicken.' I am perfectly normal. I would just as soon 'make out' as the next guy, if the girl is willing. But not with you. I like you too much for that. I probably could even fall in love with you. And make you fall in love with me. I knew that the night of the dance. But it wouldn't work out. My wife has already been selected," he added bitterly.

"By whom?" she asked.

"Oh, I don't know who she is. But I am Kenneth Jefferson Sanford the Third," he said cynically. "I will be bred with some other blue-blooded guinea pig. I will probably meet her at the shore or at some ski resort, and our families will take it from there, after they have checked every twig on each other's family tree."

"But, Kenny! In this day and age?"

"My family—and a lot like them—are still living in the Victorian era. If I don't marry the horsey debutante of their choosing, I don't get the pater's money. And I want it. I like money. Lots of it! I will never earn it on my own. So I will bow reluctantly to the family's wishes, marry, produce Kenneth Jefferson Sanford the Fourth, and then do as I please."

"What is that?" Kerry whispered.

"Race! I like racing sports cars," he answered eagerly. "What I would really like to be is a mechanic. I love cars. They are so perfect. If you take care of them, they do just as you want. They never let you down, as people do."

That is why he is so taciturn, so aloof, Kerry decided. He is afraid of forming relationships. And he doesn't want to be side-tracked. He knows what he wants out of life. Mark was right. He and Kenny *are* alike.

"So? Do you understand? Why I didn't say anything about that fracas with Ford? I figured I hadn't asked you to root for me in the first place, so why should I thank you. I don't like to be obligated to anyone."

"But, if you feel that way, why do you hang out with these kids, with the Crew?" she whispered.

"So I won't be bored. When I am bored, I get into trouble. I will tell you about that sometime."

"Hey! How about some food?" Merry's voice split the darkness.

"Not yet! After the initiation." That was Duke.

"What is the initiation?" asked Merry.

"Nothing for you to concern yourself with," answered Kenny abruptly. "Come on, let's get out of here."

But it was too late. Merry flicked on the lights. The girls sat up, combed their hair, put on fresh lipstick, while the boys gathered in a group.

"How are we going to leave now?" Kerry was impatient. If only Kenny had gone when she had asked him!

"Don't worry," he promised as he stood up. "When we leave, you get into my car. I will drive you home and come back."

"But where is everybody going?"

"We are having the initiation out—at—at—outside of town," he explained as he left to join the group.

But she didn't make it to Kenny's car. Neil and Tiger seized her by the arms as she walked down the steps and carried her off to Tiger's car. Sandwiched between them, she protested, but they ignored her.

"We pulled a fast one on our ol' buddy Sanford," chortled Neil. He threw his arm around her and pulled her towards him. She jerked away and fell against Tiger who was driving.

"Cool it, Neil! Cool it!" ordered Tiger. "How many beers did you have anyway?"

"Not beer, ol' buddy," corrected Neil. "Whisky, man, whisky! I got it outa ol' man Raleigh's liquor cabinet," he giggled. Then he began to sing and beat time with his fists on the dashboard.

"You are drunk!" Tiger said disgustedly. "Knock it off or you will get out and walk!"

Neil subsided and contented himself with pawing Kerry's shoulders. The next few minutes were an eternity for her until Tiger pulled up before an iron gate. The two boys piled out of the car, but Kerry didn't move.

"Come on, Kerry," insisted Neil. "You gonna stay here? Whatsa matter? 'Fraid of ghosts? Of lil' ol' dead people?" He wavered off unsteadily.

Dead people! She peered at the gate and the vague white and grey shapes beyond. It was the cemetery! Thoroughly frightened, she sat frozen. They were going to have their initiation in the cemetery! This wasn't kid stuff any more. This was desecration. This was a criminal offense.

"Coming, Kerry?" Tiger asked as he bent down to look into the car.

She was speechless. She could only stare at him, horror in her eyes.

"Look, it is all in fun. Nobody is going to get hurt. What are you worried about? You are not getting initiated tonight. You are only a pledge. You have to attend three parties before you are officially in the Crew."

"Hey, Tiger, what are you doing with my girl?" It was Kenny!

"Just a joke, son," Tiger laughed. "She is all yours." He hurried through the gate.

"Kerry, I am sorry, but those guys were quicker on the draw. It will be all right, though. We will stand up on the outside of the crowd and slip away in a few minutes."

"I can't—I can't—go up there!" she cried.

"*I* have to, Kerry. I am the leader; I *have* to be there. Just come up for a few minutes. Then we will disappear. I promise."

"I will—I will—stay here!" She was on the verge of tears.

"No, you won't. I won't let you stay here all by yourself in the dark! Come on!"

Reluctantly she got out and let him lead her into the cemetery. White stone figures gleamed faintly in the blackness; tall obelisks loomed up against the star-spattered sky. She had never been in a graveyard at night, but she had walked, on spring afternoons, in the one near Huron. She had always considered it a place of beauty and contented silence. But this place, at night, was macabre. Or was it the purpose for which they were trespassing that was macabre?

When they stumbled blindly to the top of a knoll, they saw the Crew gathered in front of a large mausoleum. Tiger had just jimmied the door open, and the crowd surged in after him.

"Kenny! I can't! I won't! I won't go in there!" She turned and ran.

"Come on," Kenny insisted, leading her back. "You have come this far. I told you we would skip out just as soon as they get started!"

There was no turning back so she allowed him to lead her by

the hand to the steps of the mausoleum. Everyone, with the exception of Duke and the two boys who were obviously going to be initiated, was sitting in a circle on the floor. Duke had started a fire on the marble in the middle of the group. Transfixed, Kerry stared at the leaping flames. Duke held a long piece of iron over the blaze, turning it slowly until it became red-hot. It wasn't until she saw the two boys remove their jackets and roll up their sleeves that she realized what Duke was about to do.

"He—he—he is going to brand them!" she whispered, horrified.

"Duke's idea," said Kenny. "He has been trying to top me ever since I beat him in the drag race the night of the Frolic."

Hypnotized, Kerry watched as Duke held the iron up and spit on it. The glowing metal hissed. Nonchalantly, as though he were toasting marshmallows, he returned the iron to the flames. Then, satisfied that it was hot enough, he motioned the boys to approach.

"Drop that, you idiot! What do you young fools think you are doing here?" A strange yet vaguely familiar voice shattered the silence. The words echoed and re-echoed, hollowly, in the empty vault. Duke and the two boys, like figures in a frieze, like actors in a tableau, stood motionless. Then Duke let go of the iron and it clattered to the floor.

Kerry turned to see who the intruder was. It was Doctor Sherry! He stared angrily down at the crowd. And Mark stood next to him!

"Get out!" Doctor Sherry thundered. "Get out and go home!"

He strode into the middle of the group, picked up the rod and scattered the burning wood. "Tomorrow you guys will come up here and clean up!"

Silently they got up and stole out, Indian file. Even Neil was shocked into sobriety. Only Duke remained.

"Something the matter with your hearing, Kraft?" asked the teacher.

"What right have you to tell us what to do?" Duke sneered.

"Rather have the police?" snapped Doctor Sherry, switching on a flashlight.

Duke stared insolently at him. Then he shrugged and sauntered out the door.

"Sanford? Didn't you hear me either?" the teacher asked as he noticed Kerry and Kenny standing at the top of the steps.

"He—Kenny—he didn't—he really didn't have anything to do with it," Kerry protested.

"He is here, isn't he? And so are you, Kerry. I couldn't believe it when Mark told me what you were planning."

"Mark? How did he know?" she asked.

"I overheard some of the Crew discussing it at lunch," explained Mark.

"Squealer!" muttered Kenny.

"All right. So I squealed," admitted Mark. "But, if you didn't have sense enough to keep Kerry out of this, somebody had to. I knew that she was going to the party, and I knew about the initiation. I was sure that she would not have the courage to back out. And you, Sanford, I wasn't sure about you either. So I called Doctor Sherry and asked him what to do."

He is right, Kerry thought. I did not have the courage. I

could have made Kenny take me home if I had really wanted to.

"Let's go," the teacher said, herding them down the steps to the gravel walk outside the mausoleum. "Kenny, round up the boys tomorrow and we will come back here and clean up. I will tell the cemetery superintendent and he can have the door repaired."

"The superintendent?" Kenny asked.

"You didn't think that you were going to get away with this scot-free, did you? You will have to pay for it," Doctor Sherry warned.

"Pay? How?" Kenny asked.

"Not only in money. By breaking up the Crew. You have a choice, Stanford. I will talk to the superintendent and tell him that you are willing to make restitution in any way he sees fit. I will ask him not to report it to the police, under one condition. I want all of you, and your parents, to meet with me in the high school tomorrow evening. Then you will officially disband the Crew."

The parents! *My* parents! Kerry was appalled. Mother will be so ashamed of me! And Dad! What will he do?

She found out when Doctor Sherry and Mark dropped her at her house. Her mother was ashamed of her. Although Mrs. Kendall said nothing when Kerry related the evening's experiences, it was obvious that she was disappointed in her daughter. Her father, on the other hand, did not explode angrily as she had expected. The next evening, before the meeting with Doctor Sherry, he talked with her for an hour. Chagrined and repentant, Kerry listened silently.

"This thing with the Crew, as they call themselves, is fake," he began. "This popularity, this being top dog at school, it is false, Kerry. Oh, I know that at your age you feel the need to conform, to be one of the 'haves' and not one of the 'have-nots.' I guess it is because you are not sure who or what you are, and so you try on different kinds of personalities, just the way you try new lipsticks and new hair styles. But lots of times you try on the wrong one, the wrong personality. You did. Just thank your lucky stars it wasn't any worse. If those kids hadn't been stopped, you all would have been in serious trouble."

"It was Mark and Doctor Sherry that I have to thank, really," she admitted in a low voice.

"You are right. Doctor Sherry stuck his neck out for you, for all of them. I hope you are grateful."

"I am, Dad! I am!"

"I am glad. I believe you. Now, we had better get going. The meeting is at eight o'clock," he reminded her as he left to get the car.

"I am not going," her mother said. "I have to stay with Grandma. But you will be all right now, Kerry. You are our daughter. That is all you have to remember."

Kerry kissed her mother. She looks tired, she thought. I have been selfish. All I thought about is *me*. No more, she vowed.

"Mom, I guess I grew up last night. I found out that I don't need the Crew or modeling or anything or anyone except you and Dad. And—and—Mark," she finished haltingly.

"I know. That is why Dad and I were not angry with you. We could tell. But you had better run along. Dad is waiting. And, Kerry, hurry home. I have something to tell you, something that will please you, I hope, something that perhaps I should have told you before," she said mysteriously.

CHAPTER XXII

The meeting was held in the school library. Kerry and her father were the last ones to arrive. No one spoke to anyone else. They just sat, parents and sons and daughters, staring at Doctor Sherry and two other men who were conversing in low tones at the front of the room.

At eight o'clock the two men sat down at a table; the teacher turned and looked at the group. "Is everyone here?" he asked.

"My father couldn't make it." It was Kenny. "He said—he said that he would pay for the damages." The boy sounded bitter.

"But, Kenneth, that was one of the stipulations, that you kids wouldn't be prosecuted if your parents—"

"I know, Doctor Sherry," Kenny interrupted. "But my father says that I am old enough to take care of myself, that I got into this and I have to get out of it the best way I can."

The other parents looked smugly at each other as if to say, "*We* care about our children. *We* came."

"O.K., Ken. I will talk to your father," the teacher promised.

Then he went on to explain the purpose of the meeting. He apologized for taking matters into his own hands, but, he explained, he thought a great deal of these young people, and he did not want them to be stigmatized for the rest of their lives for a foolish escapade that might have resulted in a tragedy.

"Suppose that one of the boys who was to be branded— suppose that he had suddenly jerked away when Duke was about to apply the iron? Or suppose Duke had missed. Suppose the boy had been blinded?" He waited for his words, his implications, to take effect. They did. The women's faces twisted in horror; the men's, in anger. Their sons and daughters hung their heads.

"I honestly do not think that this would have happened if your children had not been drinking. Now I am not going to deliver a temperance lecture. It is none of my business that you parents serve beer to your young guests or let your sons and daughters serve it to their friends. Or that you leave the liquor cabinet unlocked. That is your concern. But it must *be* your concern. You would not approve of providing heroin at a party for teen-agers. And yet drunken adolescents are more of a menace than dope addicts. A few drinks gives a boy false courage. He will do things that he would not dream of doing if he were sober. A few drinks do just the opposite for a girl. She *loses* her courage, the courage to say 'no.' "

The parents were shocked at his candor, but no one moved; no one spoke.

"You will have to set up your own rules for your son or daughter. But there will *have* to be rules from now on. Chief Hartford has promised that there will be no police prosecution, but he does insist upon reparation. And he has warned that the slightest deviation from the straight and narrow will result in your son being picked up. Or your daughter if she is involved. It is sort of an unofficial probation. Right, Chief? Is there anything you want to add?" He turned to the tall, grey-haired man behind him at the table.

"No, Doctor Sherry, you have said it all, much better than I could, I might add," the chief said.

"Mr. Hentzel? Did you want to say anything?" the teacher asked the other man. "Mr. Hentzel is the cemetery superintendent," he explained.

"No," he replied. "As long as they know what the boys have to do and they do it, I am satisfied. It is fortunate that the vault belongs to a family that lives in Europe, a family that hasn't been in this country for years. The damage is minor and it can be repaired. If it were serious, I might have to notify them and . . ." He shook his head.

"I would like to say something." A tall, dark-haired man rose abruptly. "I am Merry Raleigh's father. This whole thing started at our house. I cannot tell you how sorry we are."

"Gary," another father interrupted, "you are not to blame. It could have been our place or Jeff Kraft's—or any one of our homes. We are all equally guilty."

"I know that," Mr. Raleigh continued. "This is what I was about to say. We have all gone along with this. We want our children to have everything, including social status, whatever that is. We have been willing to do anything so they might achieve it. I can tell you I was pretty shocked when Merry was in eighth grade and had her first party. When my wife and I went into the living room, we found all the lights out! And these youngsters were only twelve years old! We didn't want to embarrass our daughter before her friends so we just sort of joked and turned on the lights. No sooner were our backs turned than out they went again! And, afterwards, she pleaded with us, informed us that her friends wouldn't come to our home if we—if her mother and I didn't just disappear when the party began! She told us that the other parents left the house! Left the house with those children in it all alone! It is a wonder worse things than this haven't happened!"

When he sat down, the parents looked at each other guiltily.

"That is something that you will have to talk about among yourselves, I guess," said Doctor Sherry. "That is not my affair. What we are here for tonight is to let your boys and girls know what the score is. I thought at first they should be made to break up the Crew. But now—I don't know. That is up to them and up to you."

Most of the parents nodded agreement.

"I have had it!" Tiger blurted out suddenly. "I don't want any part of the Crew anymore! A lot of us feel that way, *have* felt that way, but we didn't have the guts to say so!"

"Good for you, Tiger," Doctor Sherry said warmly. "Maybe some of the rest will have the guts, as you put it, to get out. But, whether you do or not, is your concern. I don't think there is anything more to be said tonight. I just want to apologize for taking matters into my own hands. I suppose I should get fired for—"

"Over my dead body!" exclaimed Mr. Raleigh. "I want to thank you, Doctor Sherry. I know that I speak for every single mother and father in this room when I say that I will never be able to express my gratitude for what you did!"

The other parents chorused vigorous affirmatives and crowded around the teacher to shake his hand.

"Oh, before I forget it," he announced above the hubbub, "it is Mark Lee that you really have to thank. If it had not been for Mark, I would not have known about the initiation. He is the one who really went out on a limb. The Crew thinks he squealed, and they could have—they might have been out to get him. He knew that. I even offered to go to the cemetery alone and no one would ever have known how I found out about it. But he insisted that he go along, too. There is a boy who has guts."

Kerry had sat motionless, tense, throughout the entire proceedings. Her mind was a blank. Now a warm feeling of gratitude for the teacher overwhelmed her. Tears of relief rolled unchecked down her cheeks. Embarrassed, she turned toward her father and fumbled in her bag for a handkerchief.

"He is—he is wonderful," she sniffed.

"Yes, he is," her father agreed. "I hope you all appreciate what he did for you. Actually he should have contacted Mr. Durham first, but there wasn't time. I guess Durham was too embarrassed to show up here tonight. Doctor Sherry talked to him this afternoon, and he admitted that he had been too lax as far as disciplining the Crew was concerned. He blamed it on parental pressures, and he is right. But, now he knows that he has their backing, he has promised to make the Crew—to make all the students, in fact—toe the mark. That still doesn't eliminate the fact that Doctor Sherry jeopardized his teaching job for you young people. I hope you are grateful."

"Oh, Dad, we—I am!" she answered, following him out the door. She didn't like saying "we;" she didn't want to be a part of them anymore.

"I hope, too, that they do not take it out on Mark," he worried.

"They won't, Dad. I think a lot of them agree with Tiger. I know they do! Oh, I guess there will be a few of them that will still hang out together, but it will not be the same."

"Well, I hope so. You can thank Mark personally, Kerry. He is coming over for a few minutes when we get home."

I should be happy, she thought. But I am not, not completely happy. What if Mark should tell me that he doesn't want to see me again? What if he will not, cannot forgive me? But, if he feels that way, why did he ask Doctor Sherry to stop the initiation? He *must* care about me!

When they arrived home, Mr. Kendall went to bed, explaining to his wife that Kerry would relate to her what had happened at school.

"I have been stupid and selfish, Mom," she confessed, "but from now on, I will be different. It will be just you and Dad and Grandma and me. And Mark, I hope," she said, crossing her fingers.

"And someone else," her mother said quietly.

"Someone else? Oh, you mean Andrea? I know, Mom, I have been—"

"Well, I had not thought of naming her Andrea, that is, if it is a girl."

"Mom! What are you talking about?" She stared at her mother.

"I am going to have a baby, Kerry."

"Mom! A *baby*! At your age?" she cried, thoughtlessly.

"Kerry! I am not exactly senile. I am not old!"

"I didn't mean that, Mom! I meant—oh, I don't know what I meant! It is just such a surprise!"

I can't believe it, she thought. Mother having a baby! No wonder she has been so contented lately; no wonder she has looked so glowing! And that is why Dad and Grandma have been so happy, too. That is the undercurrent I was aware of and couldn't quite understand. But, is it really true?

"Mom! Are you sure?"

"Oh, Kerry, you are—you are priceless!" Her mother laughed until the tears coursed down her cheeks. "If you—if you—had been—if you had only opened your eyes!" She hugged Kerry tight.

"I *thought* you were—were putting on weight, but I figured it was because—you know—that you were not worrying about money or because we had this beautiful house or . . ."

How blind I was, she thought ruefully. My own mother and I didn't know that she was pregnant! But why didn't they tell me before? If I had known, I would not have dragged her off to New York. I would have helped her more. But, down deep, she wasn't sure; she wasn't certain that she would have acted differently.

"Aren't you just a little bit happy?" her mother asked.

"Mom! I think it is wonderful! You *know* I do! Why didn't you tell me?"

"Dad wanted me to, as soon as I found out. But I didn't think it was fair to take you away from the excitement of modeling and all the rest of it. I thought you might be—you might feel obligated to do chores or to take care of Grandma."

Guiltily, Kerry admitted to herself that she should have been sharing more of the responsibility, even if her mother were not pregnant.

"Mom!" she said suddenly. "It might be a girl! She could share my room! That would be wonderful! To have a sister!"

"Well, I cannot guarantee *that!* It might be a boy, you know," her mother laughed.

"But where would we put a boy? If Grandma weren't here, we could use that room for a nursery." When she saw the expression on her mother's face, she realized how thoughtless, how cruel she had sounded. "I didn't mean—oh, Mom! You know I love Grandma! I only meant—"

"Kerry," her mother interrupted quietly, "Grandma's room may be empty by the time the baby arrives." Her mother's face seemed to fall apart, to shatter into lines and furrows.

"Where is she going? Dad wouldn't put her into a nursing home, would he?"

"No, the Doctor says she doesn't have long to live."

"Oh, no! I didn't know!"

"We didn't want you to, Kerry. There is nothing you can do, nothing anyone can do. She knows."

"I guess I am more ashamed of that—of paying so little attention to Grandma—than I am of anything else," Kerry admitted sorrowfully.

"She understands."

"Mom, when will the baby be born? How do you know that Grandma won't see her? Can the doctor be sure? Really sure that she—"

"We don't know for certain. I expect the baby in July, the middle of July. The doctor says Grandma—he says about the end of June."

A light tapping on the front door startled them, until Kerry remembered.

"That must be Mark. He didn't ring the bell because it is so late."

"It is late," her mother agreed. "I am going to bed. Don't stay up too late, Kerry." She kissed her daughter lightly on top of the head and went upstairs.

CHAPTER XXIII

"Come in, Mark," Kerry said formally as she opened the door.

"I will not stay long," he promised, "but I wanted to talk to you, Kerry."

He sat on the couch and Kerry sat opposite him in her father's chair. She couldn't look at him, not just yet. She started peeling polish from her thumbnail.

"I can't talk to you 'way over there, Kerry," he said softly. "Come over here and sit next to me."

Still unable to meet his eyes, she got up, walked slowly over to the couch, and sat, stiffly, on the edge of the cushion.

"Kerry, look at me," he commanded, sliding over close to her.

She turned, and, without raising her head, stole a glance at him. He made a fist and playfully, gently, jabbed her chin.

"I guess a caveman would have clobbered you over the head and dragged you off," he chided. "Maybe I should have done that long ago."

"Oh, Mark," she admitted, "I have been ten kinds of a fool!"

"That you have. That you have," he agreed. "I will not quarrel with that. But it is ancient history. And I will strangle the guy who says that history repeats itself! Not in your case, it won't!"

She leaned back into the circle of his arms. *This* was security; *this* was what she had been seeking all along. She had had it once and had almost thrown it away for the cheap glitter, the fool's gold of false popularity. This was the boy who not only loved her but was also her friend. She loved him, but, what was even more important, she *liked* him. That wasn't always true. *Love* wasn't always accompanied by *liking*. She had thought that she was in love with Tom, but she hadn't liked him particularly as a person. And Kenny. He had been, momentarily, exciting, but she disliked him in many ways.

"What are you thinking?" Mark murmured.

"That I like you," she admitted.

"Oh, so that is it! You just *like* me," he teased.

When she told him what she had been thinking about, he laughed and then said, soberly, "I imagine a lot of people don't find that out until after they are married. You did. And I did. Because I like you, too." He bent his head and kissed her lightly on the tip of her nose. "And now I had better take off. It is late."

"So soon? But I thought you said that you wanted to talk to me?" Kerry complained.

"I did. Want to, that is. But, somehow, when I am near you, I just cannot remember what I had planned to say," he teased.

"My fatal charm, no doubt," Kerry grinned.

"Indubitably. But even more fatal might be your stern male parent's forceful removal of me from the premises."

They looked at each other and laughed.

Oh, Mark, she thought, you will never know how much I love you. I will spend a lifetime trying to prove it to you.

"See you at school tomorrow," Mark said, getting up.

"See you at school," she agreed. "And reserve a table at the Hut."

"Will do. Will do," he promised as he left.

There were so many things to do, so many things to think about for the next few months—school work, college application, senior class activities, graduation, the baby, her grandmother's illness. When life seemed like a hopelessly intricate jigsaw puzzle, all bits and pieces, Kerry turned to Mark. Somehow he always helped her to fit them into their proper places.

With Doctor Sherry's assistance, she not only was admitted to his alma mater, she also received, on his recommendation, a scholarship for four years. She whirled through commencement and the other activities of graduation week. Then it was summer vacation. Although she was offered several modeling assignments, she refused them. When her mother insisted that she accept them, Kerry told her flatly that she felt that she was needed at home, that she *wanted* to be at home.

When Jamie came for a visit to the Starks' home, Mark and Kerry and Jamie and Andrea double-dated. Occasionally they met some of the Crew, at the drive-in, or at the Hut. The group, as a group, however, had disintegrated. Only Tracey had a few loyal satellites.

During the long golden June evenings, Kerry and her mother strolled about the Stanford place. Kenny and his parents had left for England for an indefinite vacation. Kerry often thought of him and hoped that the girl whom his mother and father chose for him would understand him. When she told her mother about Kenny's conversation with her at Merry's party, Mrs. Kendall merely commented, "Kenneth may never be happy, but he will be contented."

The baby was born on the Fourth of July, much to Grandma's delight. Still mentally alert, despite her physical debility, she said, feebly, when Kerry told her that her mother had gone to the hospital, "Good! No one will ever forget his birthday!"

"Or hers," Kerry said.

"Won't be a girl. A boy," Grandma answered.

Grandma was right. It was a boy, a handsome, nine-pound boy.

"I thought new-born babies were always sort of wrinkled, sort of like prunes," Kerry observed as she and her father peered through the window at the hospital nursery.

"Some of them are," her father grinned. "But not ours!"

He is so proud, Kerry thought happily. It is a wonder that he can keep his feet on the ground!

When Mrs. Kendall and the baby came home, they took him into Grandma's room immediately. She insisted that they prop her up on pillows so that she could get a good look at him.

"What did you name him?" she whispered.

"We want you to name him, Grandma," Mrs. Kendall said softly.

"Brad. Call him 'Brad.'" She closed her eyes, fell back, and slept.

The next morning Mr. Kendall woke Kerry and told her that her grandmother had died in her sleep. When she started to sob, he said, gently but firmly, "Don't cry, Kerry. She wanted to see her grandson. And she did. It made her very happy."

The funeral was a blur. Kerry remembered only the blanket of roses that her father had made to cover the grave. Always, forever after, the scent of roses saddened her a little.

But the new baby more than filled the gap left by her grand-mother's death. He was fat and healthy; he seemed to be eating constantly. Despite the fact that her mother told her that he really could not distinguish objects at so early an age, Kerry insisted that he *knew* her, that he smiled at *her,* that he was most contented in *her* arms.

She told Mark about it one evening when they were sitting on the wall at the edge of the woods behind her house.

"I guess that all females react that way to babies," he commented. "I am afraid that my interest in small fry is purely academic."

"Oh, Mark!"

"Don't worry. I shall be a fond father."

"In ten years," she said glumly.

"No, in *five* years. You are so anxious to tie me up in the bonds of holy matrimony that I have decided to marry you the day after we graduate from college."

"That is, if I have a job," she grinned.

"I warned you. No job, no wedding band." He took her left hand and wound a piece of grass around the third finger. "Maybe this will be the only one you will ever have. Maybe I won't be able to afford a gold one."

They both stared at the green circlet.

"I would even settle for that," she said.

"No Italian sports car? No trips to Europe? No mink? No diamonds?" he asked.

"No, Mark. Just you."

"Seriously, Kerry, it will not be easy. You know that. I *have* to write. There are things going on in this world that *have* to be written about. And I have to do it. That is just the way I am. And I *have* to love you. Somehow you—and my writing—they are one."

"I know, Mark," she said quietly. "Last night I read that sonnet that you told me to read last Christmas. Remember?" She reached for his hands, clasped them tightly and began softly:

> "How do I love thee? Let me count the ways.
> I love thee to the depth and breadth and height
> My soul can reach, when feeling out of sight
> For the ends of Being and ideal Grace.
> I love thee to the level of everyday's
> Most quiet need, by sun and candlelight.

I love thee freely, as men strive for Right!
I love thee purely, as they turn from Praise.
I love thee with the passion put to use
In my old griefs, and with my childhood's faith.
I love thee with a love I seemed to lose
With my lost saints,—I love thee with the breath,
Smiles, tears, of all my life!—and, if God choose,
I shall but love thee better after death." (1)

(1) Browning, Elizabeth Barrett—*Sonnets from the
Portuguese.*